Should she go to bed with Liam? Conceive his child?

No, she couldn't. It was just a mad thought conjured up by the loneliness of the night. Tears filled Samantha's eyes. She so much wanted to be a mother.

As she walked unsteadily toward his bedroom door, Samantha felt her breathing become fast and uneven. As she saw Liam's sleeping form on the bed, a quick, hot tug of excitement pulled at her heart, accompanied by a sharp sense of the awesomeness of what she was contemplating.

At her husky, slightly tremulous "Liam," he woke up instantly, his body tensing.

"Sam, what is it...? What do you want?"

He had fed her the perfect line, Samantha recognized. All she needed now was the courage to take it...use it....

"What I want, Liam, is you...." Then she placed her mouth very delicately over his.

Dear Reader,

Penny Jordan continues her dramatic family saga, THE CRIGHTONS, with *The Perfect Father*. Samantha Miller wants to find the right man and have children, like her happily married twin sister, Bobbie, whose story was told in *The Perfect Seduction*. Is there a gorgeous Crighton male waiting for Sam in England, or is her American first love the man she'll marry?

All of the books featuring the Crighton family can be read independently of each other, as each tells its own fascinating story, but if you wish to read the whole collection, then these are the novels to look for:

MIRA® Books
A PERFECT FAMILY
THE PERFECT SINNER

HARLEQUIN PRESENTS®
1941—THE PERFECT SEDUCTION
1948—PERFECT MARRIAGE MATERIAL
1954—THE PERFECT MATCH?
2025—THE PERFECT LOVER

Penny Jordan

THE PERFECT FATHER

THE CRIGHTONS

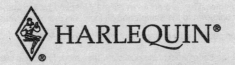

HARLEQUIN®

TORONTO • NEW YORK • LONDON
AMSTERDAM • PARIS • SYDNEY • HAMBURG
STOCKHOLM • ATHENS • TOKYO • MILAN • MADRID
PRAGUE • WARSAW • BUDAPEST • AUCKLAND

ISBN 0-373-12092-3

THE PERFECT FATHER

First North American Publication 2000.

Copyright © 2000 by Penny Jordan.

Visit us at www.romance.net

Printed in U.S.A.

The Crighton Family

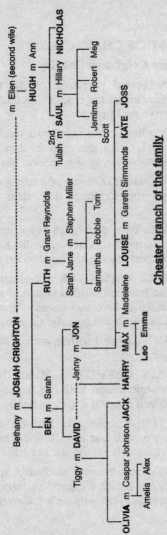

Haslewich branch of the family

Bethany m **JOSIAH CRIGHTON** ----------------- m Ellen (second wife)

HUGH m Ann

BEN m Sarah — **RUTH** m Grant Reynolds — **SAUL** m Hillary **NICHOLAS**

2nd Tullah m Scott

Jemima Robert Meg

Jenny m **JON**

Sarah Jane m Stephen Miller

Samantha Bobbie Tom

Tiggy m **DAVID** ----------------- **HARRY** **MAX** m Madeleine **LOUISE** m Gareth Simmonds **KATE JOSS**

Leo Emma

OLIVIA m Caspar Johnson **JACK**

Amelia Alex

Chester branch of the family

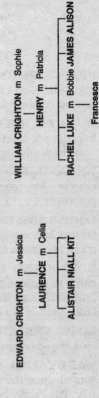

EDWARD CRIGHTON m Jessica

LAURENCE m Celia

ALISTAIR NIALL KIT

WILLIAM CRIGHTON m Sophie

HENRY m Patricia

RACHEL LUKE m Bobbie **JAMES ALISON**

Francesca

CAST OF CHARACTERS
The Crighton Family

BEN CRIGHTON: Proud patriarch of the family, a strong-minded character in his eighties, determined to see his dynasty thrive and prosper.

RUTH REYNOLDS: Ben's sister, a vibrant woman now happily reunited with Grant, the man from whom she was tragically separated during the Second World War.

JON AND JENNY CRIGHTON: Steady, family-oriented couple. Jon keeps the Crighton law firm running smoothly.

LOUISE AND KATE: Twin daughters of Jon and Jenny. Louise is happily married to Gareth, while Kate feels more and more isolated among all the married couples.

BOBBIE AND LUKE CRIGHTON: American Bobbie came to expose the truths in Ruth's past, and stayed in England when she fell in love and married charismatic Luke, part of the Chester branch of the Crighton family.

JAMES CRIGHTON: Luke's brother, successful, good-looking—and single.

MADDY AND MAX CRIGHTON: Maddy has blossomed since the reconciliation with her husband, Max, who has finally proved himself a loving, family man.

SAMANTHA MILLER: Searching for happiness in marriage, she has come to visit her twin, Bobbie, hoping to find a gorgeous Crighton husband for herself.

LIAM CONNOLLY: He's known Samantha since she was a gangly teenager—with a gigantic crush on him. He needs to understand just why he's followed her to England.

CHAPTER ONE

'THAT was some game you played over the weekend, Sam. I certainly never expected to see the Corporation's gold trophy go to a woman...'

'Sam isn't a woman, women are small and cute and cuddly, they stay at home and make babies.... Sam...even her *name* isn't womanly...'

Samantha Miller drew herself up to her full height—an inch over six feet—which was an impressive four inches above the man who had just so publicly and cruelly criticised her.

'You know your trouble don't you, Cliff,' she drawled affably. '*You* just don't know a *real* woman when you see one. Seems to me that a man isn't so very much of a man if the only kind of woman he can handle is the kind you've just described, and as for making babies...' She paused for emphasis, well aware of the fact that she had the attention of their fellow employees who had happened to be in the large airy open-plan office with them, 'I'm woman enough to have a baby any time I want one.'

Only now was she revealing the true extent of her anger at the way Cliff had insulted her; her eyes flashing challenging sparks, her voice trembling a little with the force of her feelings.

'*You* have a baby...' her antagonist jeered angrily before she could continue. 'Who the hell would want to impregnate a woman like you? No way. Your only chance of having a child would be via some med student's sperm and a syringe...'

7

Enough of the people standing around broke into laughter for Samantha to recognise that no matter how publicly she might be accepted by her colleagues, an uncomfortable proportion of them seemed to share Cliff Marlin's views.

Faced with the same situation another woman might have burst into tears or lost her temper but not Sam. You learned young when you were as tall as she was that crying didn't look cute, and besides...

Looking down from the advantage of her extra inches Samantha bared her teeth in a totally false smile and gave a dismissive shrug.

'You're entitled to your opinion, Cliff, but gee, it's a shame that you're such a sore loser. Mind, if *I* played golf as badly as you do, I guess I might be a tad sore about it, too. And as for making babies...*how* many times did you miss that putt on the eighth...'

Now it was Samantha's gibe that earned a responsive titter of amusement from around her.

Without giving Cliff the opportunity to retaliate she turned on her heel and walked quickly away, her head held high.

What did it matter that she knew the moment she was out of sight and earshot that the others would be talking about her, gossiping about her, the six foot Amazon of a woman who, in all the time she had been with the Corporation, had never attended any of its social events with an escort; the only one of her admittedly relatively small group of female peers in what was essentially a very male-biased industry who had not, at one point or another, confided the details of her private life to the others.

Now, at just over thirty, Samantha was well aware that she had entered a decade which might prove to be one of the most productive and fast-paced of her whole life. It was also a decade which would see the chance of her meeting a man, the man…the man she would be able to fall in love with, the man she would want to spend the rest of her life with, the man with whom she would have the babies she craved so much, sharply declining.

There would be men of course…were men…masses of them, men who didn't want to commit, men who didn't want children, men who did want children, but who most definitely did not want a wife, men who were already married…men who… Oh, yes, the list of men to avoid was endless and the choice narrowed even further when one was as picky as her.

'Why don't you at least have a date with him?' her twin sister Roberta had demanded the last time she had been over visiting her family in the States from her new-found home in England. Their mother had been complaining to Bobbie about Sam's obduracy in not accepting a date from the man who had been pursuing her at the time.

'There isn't any point. I already *know* he isn't the one,' Samantha had told her fatalistically. 'It's all very well for you to take Mom's side,' she had complained to her twin later when they were on their own. 'You've *found* your man, your perfect "one and only," and when I've seen how special what you and Luke have together is, how happy *you* are, how could *I* possibly settle for anything less.'

'Oh, Sam.' Bobbie had hugged her contritely. 'I'm sorry, you're right, you *mustn't* but I have to say I hope you find him soon. Oh dear,' she had then apologised as she'd started to yawn, 'I do feel tired.'

'Tired, I'm not surprised,' Samantha had laughed, and then unable to stop herself she glanced with rueful envy at her twin's heavily pregnant body—not with twins as Bobbie had first hoped, though. This was another single pregnancy. Seeing the look in her eyes Bobbie had asked her gently, 'Have you *never* met anyone you could love, Sam? Has there *never* been anyone you have loved?'

Samantha had thought for a moment before shaking her head. Her blonde hair, unlike her twin's, was cropped into a mass of short tender curls that framed her perfectly shaped face making her large blue eyes seem even larger and darker than Bobbie's.

'No. Not unless you count that crush I had on Liam way back when he first started working for Dad... I must have been all of fourteen at the time and Liam pretty soon made it clear that he wasn't interested in a juvenile brat with braces on her teeth and her hair in plaits.'

Roberta had laughed. Liam Connolly was their father's most senior assistant and it was no secret in the family that Stephen Miller was encouraging him to run for the position of State Governor when he himself retired.

'Yeah, well I guess to a man of twenty-one, especially one as good-looking as Liam, the idea of having a four-teen-year-old adoringly worshipping him doesn't hold that much appeal.'

'Believe me, so far as Liam was concerned it didn't have *any* appeal,' Sam had returned feelingly. 'Do you know he even refused to kiss me one particular Thanksgiving. Can you believe that—and me his boss's daughter...'

'Yeah, that could have been a real bad career move,' Bobbie had agreed tongue-in-cheek, '*and* an even worse one if Dad had found out Liam was encouraging you.'

'Mmm...and Liam has always put his career ahead of everything else.'

Bobbie had raised her eyebrows a little at the critical note in her twin's voice, inviting an explanation of Sam's acidic one.

'Oh, come on, Bo Bo, there's been a succession of women in his life—and his bed—but even Dad's commented on the fact he's never come anywhere near making a serious commitment to anyone. Lordy, he hasn't even allowed any of them to move into his house.'

'Perhaps he's still looking for Ms. Right...'

Samantha had given her sister an old-fashioned look.

'If he is, then all I can say is that he surely is having one hell of a good time with an awful lot of Ms. Wrongs first!'

Now, all too well aware of what was likely to be being said about her behind her back in the general office, Samantha headed for the elevators. So what if officially she wasn't due to take her lunch break for another full half an hour? Right now she needed to breathe fresh clean air and not the stale rancid stuff she had just been forced to endure, contaminated as it had been by Cliff's malice and envy. Because that *was* what had sparked his attack on her, Samantha knew that... He had been riding her hard for the last six weeks—ever since she had been offered the promotion he himself had wanted.

She had a month's leave coming up soon, thank goodness, and she had already made arrangements to spend most of it in England with her twin.

Her father's term as State Governor had only a little more time to run, otherwise he and her mother would have been joining her.

Theirs was a very close family, made all the more so because of its history. Her mother had been born illegitimately to Ruth Crighton, the unmarried daughter of the Crighton family of Haslewich in Cheshire, England, at the time when unmarried girls of Ruth's class simply did not become pregnant or certainly were not supposed to.

It had been during the Second World War. Ruth had

fallen deeply in love with Samantha's grandfather but, due
to a misunderstanding and the disapproval of her own
father who had a bias against Americans, Ruth had erro-
neously believed that Grant had lied to her about being
single and actually already had a wife and a child in the
States. Pressured by her family, Ruth had given her baby,
Samantha and Roberta's mother, up for adoption.

By one of those quirks of fate that always seemed too
far-fetched to be possible, Ruth's baby had been adopted
in secret by Grant, who had assumed that Ruth was rejecting her child in the same way she had rejected him.

It had only been when, on realising how badly their
mother, Sarah Jane, was still affected by the dreadful hurt
caused to her by *her* mother's rejection, that Samantha
and Roberta had hatched a plan to bring Ruth to book for
her desertion of her child. It was then that the whole real
circumstances surrounding the birth had come to light.

Not only had their grandparents been reunited, but
Roberta had also met Luke to whom she was now married
and already had one child. Another was on the way.

Like their grandmother, Luke, too, was a Crighton.
Only from the Chester, not the Haslewich branch of the
family.

Crightons and the law went together like peaches and
cream and so it was no surprise that Luke should be one
of the city's leading counsel.

Initially Samantha had been inclined to be a little in
awe of her slightly austere brother-in-law, but beneath that
austerity lay hidden a wicked sense of humour and a very
dry wit. True, he had stolen away Sam's beloved twin
sister and put the width of the Atlantic between them, but
he had also, it had to be admitted, made Bobbie deliri-
ously happy and they were not the kind of twins who
needed to live in one another's pockets. But there were

times like now when the one person, the only person, she
wanted was her twin sister.

Cliff Marlin might be little more than a pathetic apology for a real man but he was a pathetic apology for a
real man who had hurt her far more badly than she wanted
him or anyone else to see.

His malicious taunt had cut deep and dirty. Not even
Bobbie knew how gut-wrenchingly envious Sam sometimes felt or how shocked she had been to recognise how
strong her own inner conviction that she would be the
first one of them to marry and have children had been.

She did not begrudge Bobbie her happiness, of course
she didn't, and she had seen the anguish and pain Bobbie
had gone through when she had thought that Luke didn't
return her feelings, it was just that... It was just what?
she asked herself tersely, worrying at the thought with the
same intensity she was worrying at her bottom lip as she
strode out into the spring sunshine.

It was just that she had this *yearning,* this *hunger* to be
a mother. It was just that she felt raw with the pain of not
fulfilling the tender nurturing side of her nature. But how
could she compromise? How could she have a child when
there was no man in her life?

Earlier when Bobbie had teased her that she would have
to hurry up and find someone so that she could provide
her own baby with cousins, Sam had laughed and mocked
her twin that a man wasn't necessary for the purpose of
procreation any more, at least, not the kind of loving personal contact with one that Bobbie seemed to be enjoying
so much. She hadn't meant it of course, she had simply
been giving in to that slightly offbeat side of her nature
that had gotten her into trouble so many, many times
when she had been growing up. There was an impetuous,
an impulsive and very strong streak of determination run-

ning through her character, Samantha acknowledged
wryly.

Back there in the office just now for instance, the temptation to throw Cliff's words back at him and tell him that
she would prove to him just how much of a woman she
was, that she would prove to them all just how easily she
could find herself a partner, have herself a baby, had almost been too strong for her to resist, but fortunately she
had resisted it.

It would have been foolhardy in the extreme for her—
a career woman who worked in the hard-nosed business
of modern computer technology, where logic was a ne-
cessity—to give in to the impulse to throw caution to the
winds and go with the heady wave of emotion which had
stormed her, riding its crest triumphantly like Pacific surf
as she told Cliff that not only could she disprove his
words but that she actually would.

Naturally it ill behoved the daughter of the State's
Governor to give in to such a hotheaded impulse. Her
father was another mark against her in Cliff's eyes, of
course. She had overheard the sneering comments he had
made to another colleague when she had been offered the
job he had tried so desperately hard to win for himself.

'It's obvious she wouldn't have had a chance if it
hadn't been for the fact that her father is the State
Governor,' she had heard him saying bitterly. 'No prizes
for guessing just what's going on. The company has put
in tenders for government work and what better way to
tip the odds in their favour than by getting in the
Governor's good books by promoting his daughter...'

It wasn't true, Samantha knew that. She had *won* that
promotion on *merit*. She was, quite simply, the better person for the job and she had told Cliff so in no uncertain
terms. He hadn't liked hearing her saying it, no sirree, and

he had liked it even less when she had beaten him hands down in the firm's annual golf tournament.

She had Liam to thank for that. He was a first-rate player and, even as a teenager, he had never allowed her the indulgence of beating him, mercilessly telling her just where she was going wrong. He was equally good at playing chess—and poker—which was why her father claimed he would make a first-rate Governor.

Her parents had been discussing that very subject when they had all sat down to supper earlier in the week.

'Well, I can understand why you're so keen that Liam should run for Governor when you retire,' her mother had agreed, 'but if he gets elected he's going to be the youngest Governor this state has ever had.'

'Mmm…he's thirty-seven, which I guess does make him a little on the young side.'

'Thirty-seven and unmarried,' Sarah Jane had persisted. 'He'd stand a far better chance of getting in if he had a wife…'

As Stephen Miller raised his eyebrows, Sam's mother had insisted, 'Don't look at me like that. You *know* it's true. Voters like the idea of their Governor being a happily married family man. It makes them feel secure and it reinforces their instinctive beliefs that…'

'…that what? A married man is a better Governor than an unmarried one?' her father had asked dryly. But he still had to concede that Sarah Jane had a point.

'Well, Liam certainly isn't short of suitable candidates for the position of his wife,' her father had admired, immediately looking a little shamefaced as her mother had expostulated.

'Stephen Miller, I do believe you are envious of him!'

'Envious. No, of course I'm not,' he had protested.

'Well, I should think you should look a mite ashamed,'

her mother scolded mock severely. 'Otherwise I might start to believe that you don't appreciate either me or your family.'

'Honey, you know that just isn't true,' her father had responded immediately and so tenderly that tears had filled Samantha's eyes.

How could she ever accept second-best when she had before her not just the example of her twin's fervently happy marriage, but that of her darling, wonderful parents and, of course, her grandparents who were still just as much in love with one another now as they had been that fateful war-torn summer they had first met.

Only she seemed unable to find a mate for herself, a mate who would love her and father the children Cliff had so hatefully taunted her that no man would want to give her.

Oh, but *what* she would give to prove him wrong, to walk into that general office not just with her wonderful Mr. Right on her arm but with her stomach triumphantly, wonderfully big with his child...his children... As yet Bobbie hadn't followed in the Crighton family tradition and conceived twins. She had hoped earlier on in her current pregnancy she might have done, but her routine scans had shown that there was only one baby, although now in the late stages of her pregnancy Bobbie was grumbling that she felt large enough to be carrying quads.

Twins!

Twins... They ran through the history of the Crighton family like an often-repeated refrain and yet, oddly, despite all the new marriages which had taken place these last few years amongst her cousins—first, seconds and thirds—no one had, as yet, produced the next generation of double births.

Samantha closed her eyes. She could see herself now,

leaning a little heavily onto the strong supporting arm of her love, her smile beatific, her body weighed down by the twin babies she was carrying perhaps, but her spirits, her heart, buoyed up with love and excitement.

'Sam.'

The sharp warning note in her twin's voice was so clear, so real, that Bobbie could almost have been there beside her.

Guiltily she opened her eyes and then realised that someone *had* actually spoken to her but that that someone was most definitely not her beloved twin sister.

Exhaling warily she looked up into the silver-grey eyes of Liam Connolly.

Yes, looked *up* because Liam, thanks, or so he said, to the Viking ancestry he claimed he possessed through his mother's Norwegian family and in spite of his quite definitely un-Nordic very dark hair, was actually a good three inches taller than she was herself, taller even than her own father—just.

'Er, L—Liam…' Why on earth was she stuttering and stammering like a child caught with her fingers in a forbidden cookie jar? Samantha wondered.

Liam indicated the busy road in front of them and told her dryly, 'I *know* you like to *think* you're super-human but somehow I don't think the right way to try to prove it is to cross the freeway with your eyes closed. Besides, we have a law in this state against jaywalking, you know.'

As Sam heaved a small rebellious sigh, she had no idea what it was about Liam that always made her feel as though she was still fourteen years old and hot-headedly troublesome with it, but somehow or other he always did.

'Dad says you've agreed to run for State Governor when he retires,' she announced, trying to change the subject.

'Mmm...' He shot her a perceptive look from those incredible eyes that sometimes could seem so sexily smoky and smouldering and at other times could look so flintily cold that they could turn your heart to ice and your conscience to a clear piece of Perspex with every small sin clearly visible through it.

'I take it you don't approve?'

'You're thirty-seven. New Wiltshire County practically runs itself. I should have thought you'd want something you could get your teeth into a little more.'

'Like what? President?' Liam drawled. 'New Wiltshire County might not mean much to *you*, but believe me it's got a hell of a lot going for it. Do you realise that we're well on our way to passing new state legislation which will actually have our people voluntarily giving up their guns? Did you know that *we* have one of the lowest rates of unemployment in the entire union and that our kids have one of the *highest* overall pass out grades from high school? Did you know that our welfare programme has just been applauded as one of the finest in the union and that...'

'Yes...Yes, I *do* know all those things, and I'm not knocking the county. It's my home, after all, and I love it. My father is its Governor and...'

Fixing his steel-grey gaze on her, Liam ignored what she was saying, demanding seriously, 'Did you know that the gardens surrounding the Governor's residence have been declared a tribute to our Governor's lady's taste and knowledge of—'

'Oh, but *I* designed those,' Sam began and then stopped, glaring accusingly at him.

'Oh, all right, you got me there,' she acknowledged ruefully, her own mouth curving into a reluctant smile as she saw the humour in the curl of Liam's mouth.

'New Wiltshire County is a wonderful place, Liam, I know that. I just thought you might prefer something a little bit more...a little bit less parochial,' she told him dryly, unable to resist adding, 'After all, you seem to spend an awful lot of time in Washington.'

'With your father,' Liam replied promptly before adding, 'but if I'd realised that you were missing me...'

Sam gave him a withering look.

'Don't give *me* that,' she warned him. 'I know you— remember... I don't know what all those girls you date see in you Liam—' she began severely.

'No?' he interrupted her swiftly. 'Want me to show you?'

To her own irritation Sam could feel herself starting to colour up a little.

She knew perfectly well that Liam was only teasing her. She ought to; after all, he had been doing it for long enough.

'No thanks,' she responded automatically. 'I prefer exclusivity in my men. Exclusivity and *brown* eyes,' she told him mock musingly. 'Yes, there is quite definitely something about a man with brown eyes.'

'Brown eyes... Mmm... Well, I guess I could always keep mine closed—or wear contact lenses. What were you thinking about when I saw you just then?' he demanded, completely changing tack.

'Thinking about?'

Samantha knew perfectly well how he would read it if she was to tell him. He would be even more disapproving and dismissive than her twin sister.

'Er...nothing...not really,' she fibbed, then as she saw him start to frown and guessed that he wasn't going to let her answer stand without some further questioning, she added quickly, 'I was thinking about my upcoming visit to Bobbie.'

'You're going to England?'

Samantha shot him an uncertain look. He was frowning and his voice had sharpened almost to the point of curtness.

'Uh-huh, for a whole month. More than long enough I guess for Bobbie to put her matchmaking plans into practice,' she told him flippantly.

'Bobbie's trying to matchmake for you?'

'You know what she's like.' Samantha shrugged. 'She's so besotted with Luke that she wants to see me equally happily married off. You'd better watch out, Liam,' she joked, 'You're even older than me. She could be matchmaking for you next! Mind you, perhaps she's right. England could be the place to find a man,' Samantha mused, her eyes clouding as she remembered Cliff's taunt. 'There is something deeply attractive about English men.'

'Especially when they've got brown eyes?' Liam asked in an unfamiliarly hard voice.

'Umm...especially then,' Samantha agreed unseriously. But Liam, it seemed, was taking the subject much more seriously than she was because he looked away from her and when he looked back his eyes were a particularly cold and analytical shade of grey.

'It wouldn't be *one* specific brown-eyed Englishman we are talking about, would it?'

'One specific...' Samantha was lost. 'Well, gee, I guess one would be enough,' she agreed, putting on her best country-cousin hill-billy voice. 'At least to start with, but then... What are you getting at, Liam?' she asked him, dropping the fake accent as she saw the way he was watching her.

'I was just remembering the way Luke's brother was

watching you at Luke and Bobbie's wedding,' he told her coolly. '*His* eyes were brown, if I remember correctly.'

'James...' Samantha frowned. She couldn't quite remember what colour his eyes had been and most certainly James had been a real honey, seriously good-looking and seriously open about his own desire to settle down and raise a family, no commitment phobia there and most definitely no bias against tall independent women. No sirree.

'Mmm...you're right, they *were,*' she agreed, giving Liam an absent smile.

'Of course, we'd have brown-eyed babies.'

'*What* did you say...'

Vaguely, Samantha looked at Liam. She had just had *the* most wonderful idea.

'Brown-eyes genes dominate over blue, don't they?' she asked him, not expecting a response.

'Sam, just what the hell is going on?'

Liam grabbed hold of her upper arm, not painfully but firmly enough for Samantha to recognise that he wasn't easily going to let go of her.

She gave a small sigh and looked up at him.

'Liam, would *you* say that I was the kind of woman who couldn't...who a man wouldn't...' She stopped as her throat threatened to clog with tears, swallowing them down fiercely before continuing gruffly, 'Someone told me today that I'm not woman enough for a man to want her to...to...to become a mother. Well, I'm going to prove him wrong, Liam... I'm going to prove him so wrong that...

'I'm going to go to England and I'm going to find myself a man who *knows* how to love and value a *real* woman, the *real* woman in me and he's going to love me and I'm going to love him so much that...

'Let me go, Liam,' she demanded, aware that he'd

tightened his grip on her. 'I've already overrun my lunch hour and I've got about a million and one things I have to do...'

'Samantha,' Liam began warningly, but she'd already pulled free of him and was walking away. Her mind was made up even if rather ironically it had taken Liam of all people to point her in the right direction and there was no way she was going to let anyone change it. In England she would find love just as her twin had done. Why on earth hadn't *she* thought of that...realised that before? English men were different. English men weren't like Cliff. English men... One Englishman would love her as she so longed to be loved and she would love him right back.

Already she was regretting having told Liam as much as she had. Oh, that wilful impetuous tongue of hers, but she certainly wasn't going to tell anyone else—not even Bobbie. No, her quest to find her perfect Mr. Right, the perfect father for the babies she so longed to have, was going to be *her* secret and hers alone.

Her eyes sparkling with elation, Samantha walked back into her office building.

CHAPTER TWO

'JUST think, in a little over a week I shall be in Haslewich with Bobbie.'

Samantha closed her eyes and smiled in delicious anticipation, looking more like the teenager she had been when Liam had first met her than the sophisticated, independent career woman she now was.

On the opposite side of the elegant mahogany dining table, which was a family heirloom and which her mother had insisted on bringing with them from the family residence in the small town which her husband's family had virtually founded to the Governor's residence where they now all lived together, Sarah Jane Miller smiled tenderly at her daughter.

'I really do envy you, darling,' she told her. 'I just wish that your father and I were coming with you but it's impossible right now.'

'I know, but at least you'll be getting to spend Christmas with Bobbie this year. Dad's term of office will have finished by then.'

'Mmm... I must admit I shan't be sorry,' her mother responded, and then looked apologetically across the table to the fourth member of the quartet.

Over the years Liam Connolly had worked for her husband the two men had become very close and Sarah Jane knew it was no secret to Liam that she preferred the elegant New England home she had shared with her husband to the rather less intimate atmosphere of the

Governor's residence which was also home to the state's small suite of administration offices.

'Oh, Liam, it's not that the house isn't…' She stopped and laughed, shaking her head. 'What am I saying,' she chuckled ruefully. '*You* know all too well that I can't wait to get back to our own home. I hope that when you do decide to marry that you'll warn your wife-to-be just what she's going to have to take on…when she moves in here…'

'It isn't a foregone conclusion that I'll get elected to the governorship,' Liam reminded her dryly.

'Oh, but I hope you do,' Samantha's mother insisted. 'You're so obviously the very best man for the job.'

'Sarah Jane is right,' Samantha's father cut in warmly. 'And I can tell you, Liam, that I've heard on the grapevine that the New Wiltshire and even some Washington hostesses are already preparing their celebratory dinners for you.'

Dutifully Samantha joined in her mother's amused laughter but for some reason she couldn't define, she didn't find the idea of Liam being vetted by the sophisticated women of Washington as pleasantly amusing as both her parents did.

'There is one thing you are going to have to consider though, Liam,' her father was continuing in a more serious vein. 'I'm not saying that your election to the governorship is dependent on it, but there's no getting away from the fact that as a married man you would significantly increase your appeal to the voters.'

Very carefully Liam put the pear he had been peeling back on his plate. He had, Samantha noticed, unlike her, managed to remove most of its skin without either drastically altering the shape of the fruit or covering himself in its juice. But then, Liam was like that. She had seen him remove his suit jacket to set about lending a hand to some mundane task requiring the kind of muscle power so very evident in his six-foot-four broad-shouldered frame and complete the job without even managing to get a speck of dirt on his immaculately clean shirt. She, on the other hand, couldn't so much as open a fridge door without knocking something over.

'It's only a matter of months before voting takes place,' Liam reminded her father dryly. 'Somehow I feel that the voters would be less than impressed by a hasty and a very obviously publicity-planned marriage.'

'There's plenty of time before your first term of office would begin,' her father pointed out. 'I knew I wanted to marry Sarah Jane within days of first meeting her.'

Across the table Samantha's parents exchanged tenderly loving looks. Sam looked away. Her parents were so very, very lucky.

Fiercely she worried at her lip. As a teenager her mother had once told her gently, chidingly, 'Samantha Miller, if you keep on doing that, that poor bottom lip of yours is going to be permanently sore and swollen.'

'Mom's right,' Bobbie had hissed teasingly at her when their mother had left the room. 'But my, oh, my, how sexy it's going to look. Boys are just going to die wanting to feel how it is to kiss you.'

'Boys…yuck…' Samantha had protested. Who wanted boys when there was *Liam?* What would it be like to be kissed by him? He had the sexiest mouth she had ever seen. Just thinking about it, never mind looking at it, made her shiver all over.

'I understand what you're saying,' Liam was admitting to her father now, 'but personally I don't believe that getting married is necessarily going to make me a better Governor. In fact,' he added wryly, 'it would probably be more likely to have just the opposite effect. Men in love are, after all, notoriously unable to concentrate upon anything other than their beloved.'

'Perhaps it's just as well then that you are in love with your career,' Samantha suggested, adding before Liam could comment, 'You have to admit that you've always given it far more attention than you have any woman.'

'Sam...' her mother objected, but Liam simply shook his head.

'No wonder you're no good at chess,' he taunted her, 'making a move on your opponent is no good unless you keep yourself protected and have the next move already planned. *I* could point out that you are equally bereft of a partner and that you, too, would appear to have sacrificed your most personal intimate relationships in favour of your career.'

'Not in the way that you have, I haven't,' Samantha objected hotly. 'You deliberately pick women who you know you're going to get bored with. You don't want a serious relationship. You're a commitment phobic, Liam,' she told him dangerously. 'Secretly you're afraid of giving yourself emotionally to a woman.'

'Oh, then it seems to me that we have something very much in common.'

'What do you mean?' Samantha asked him challengingly.

'It's so obvious that the kind of man you need is one who'd keep you earthed, provide a solid base to offset your own more tempestuous one, but instead you always go for the same type, emotionally unstable, manipulative, lame dogs. My guess is you feel more passionate about them as a cause than as men.

'You accuse me of being afraid of giving myself emotionally to a woman, Samantha. Well I'd say that you are very much afraid of committing yourself, of giving yourself wholly and completely, sexually, to a man. Excuse me.' Without giving her any opportunity to either defend herself or retaliate, he stood up, politely excusing himself to her parents.

'I've got some work I really need to do. I'll see you in the morning Stephen and I should have those figures you were asking me for by then.'

As he walked around the table and gave her mother a brief kiss on the cheek Samantha wondered if her face looked as hot with chagrin as it felt. How could he have said something like that to her, and in front of her parents? It wasn't true, of course, how could it be?

It wasn't, after all, as though she was some timid, cowering virgin who had never known physical intimacy. She had lost her virginity in the time-honoured way as a sophomore at college with her then boyfriend whom she had been dating for several months. And if the experience had turned out to be more of a rite of passage than the entry into a whole new world of perfect love and emotional and physical bliss and euphoria, well then she hadn't been so very different from any of her peers, from what she had heard.

True that, unlike Liam, she didn't have a list of sexual conquests as long as her arm. True, her own secret, somewhat mortifying view of herself was as a woman to whom sex was never going to be of prime importance, certainly nothing as important as emotional intimacy or as the love she would have for the children she would bear. But was that so very wrong? Did putting sex at the top of one's list of what was important in life truly make for a better person? Samantha didn't think so and she was certainly not going to pretend to either a sexual desire or a sexual

history she did not possess simply because it might be
expected of her.

'You know, it's at times like this that I wonder if you're
actually a teenager or really in your thirties,' Samantha
heard her father remark ruefully as he, too, stood up.

Imploringly she looked at her mother.

'That's not fair, Mom. It was *Liam* who started it
and...'

'Your father does have a point, darling,' her mother
interrupted her gently. 'You *do* tend to ride Liam rather
hard at times.'

'*I* ride *him!*' Samantha objected indignantly, and then
she suddenly felt her face flooding with scarlet colour, not
because she felt guilty about what she had said but because she had suddenly realised the sexual connotations
of her mother's comment.

Liam...sex...and her? Oh no! No... She had outgrown
that particular folly a long time ago.

'He deserves it,' she told her mother fiercely. 'He can
be so damned arrogant. If he ever gets to be Governor
he's going to have to develop a far more human and gentle way of dealing with other people. When it comes to
figures or logic Liam may be the best there is, but when
it comes to his fellow human beings...'

'Sam. Now you *are* being unfair,' her mother chided
her firmly. 'And I think you know it. If you'd only seen
the way Liam reacted to and spoke with the children at
the Holistic Centre the other week.'

She paused and shook her head.

'I could have sworn I saw tears in his eyes when he
was holding that little boy,' she commented to her husband as he prepared to leave the room. 'You remember

the one I mean, the autistic boy they had there for assessment.'

'Yes, Liam told me himself that if he gets elected he intends to make sure that the centre gets the very best of funding and help he can give it.'

The Holistic Centre was one of Sam's mother's pet charities—the establishment and support of charities was very much a Crighton thing on the other side of the Atlantic. The series of special units Ruth, Samantha's grandmother and Sarah Jane's mother, had established were unique in the facilities they provided for single parents and their children and all the Crighton women were tireless in their fund-raising work for a diverse range of good causes.

Out of all the charities her own mother supported, the Holistic Centre, which treated children with special needs, was Samantha's own favourite and whenever she could she gave her spare time to helping out there and working to raise money for it.

'I didn't know that Liam had visited the centre,' she commented sharply now.

'Mmm... He asked if he could come with me the last time I visited,' her mother explained. 'And I must say, I was impressed with the way he related to the children. For a man without younger siblings and no children of his own, he certainly has a very sure and special touch with kids.'

'He's probably practising his baby kissing techniques to impress the voters!'

'Samantha!' her mother objected, quite obviously shocked.

'Samantha? Samantha what?' Sam demanded shakily as she got up. She knew she was overreacting and perhaps even behaving a little unfairly but somehow she couldn't help herself. Right now *she* was the one who needed her parents' support, their complete and full approval…their understanding. Cliff's cruel comments had hurt her very deeply, shaken her, disturbed her, uncovered a secret ache of unhappiness and dissatisfaction with herself and her life.

'You always take Liam's side,' she accused her bewildered parents, her eyes suddenly brilliant with tears. 'It's not fair…' And then, like the youthful teenager her father had accused her of resembling, she turned and fled from the room.

'What on earth was all that about?' Stephen asked in confusion when she had gone. 'Is it one of those women's things…?'

'No. It's not that.' Sarah Jane shook her head, her forehead pleating in an anxious maternal frown.

'I'm worried about Samantha, Stephen. I *know* she's always been inclined to be a little up and down emotionally—she's so passionate and intense about everything— but that's what makes her the very special person she is… But, well…this last year…' She paused, her frown deepening. 'I'm glad she's going on this visit with Bobbie. She never says it, but I know how much she misses her.' She paused and gave him a wry smile.

'Do you remember when they were growing up how it was always Sam who played big sister to the other kids on the block and how, when Tom came along she fussed over him like a little mother? We always said then that Sam would be the one to get married first and have children and that Bobbie would be the career girl.'

She saw that Stephen was looking a little nonplussed.

'What is it you're trying to say?' he asked her.

'I'm not sure,' she admitted. 'I just know that something's upsetting Samantha.'

'Well, she and Liam have never exactly seen eye to eye.'

'No, it isn't Liam,' Sarah Jane told him positively. 'Poor Liam, I do feel for him.' She gave a small chuckle. 'I rather suspect that if he hadn't been sitting at our dinner table there was a moment this evening when he might definitely have reacted more forcefully to Sam's remarks.'

'Mmm… He and Sam have never got on,' her husband agreed.

Sarah Jane's eyes widened.

'Oh, but…' she began and then stopped. 'Do you think he'll seriously consider getting married in order to strengthen his position in running for Governor?'

'Not purely for that,' Stephen announced positively. 'He's far too honest—and too proud—to stoop to those kinds of tactics, but like I said earlier, he is thirty-seven and, despite all the hassle Sam gives him about his girl-friends, he's never given me the impression that he's the kind of man who needs to feed his ego with a constant stream of sexual conquests—far from it.'

'Mmm… I think you're right. In fact—' She stopped. 'With his ancestry it's entirely feasible that Liam's rational exterior could hide a very emotional and romantic heart indeed. In fact I think that Liam, contrary to what Sam said, *is* looking for love and commitment—he just hasn't found the right woman yet, that's all.'

She got up from the table and dropped a loving kiss on her husband's cheek as she walked past him.

'I'd better go up and see if Sam's okay.'

A week later Samantha gave a small sigh of achievement and relief as the clasps on her large suitcase finally responded to the pressure of her weight on top of the case and snapped closed.

'Thank goodness,' Sam muttered under her breath.

She would be way over the weight limit, she *knew* that, but what the heck. A series of long excited conversations with her twin over the intervening week had elicited the information that there were a series of social events coming up in both Chester and Haslewich which Bobbie intended to have her twin join in.

'There's the Lord Lieutenant's Ball at the end of your stay. We've already got tickets for that. It's going to be especially wonderful this year as the current Lord Lieutenant is stepping down. You'll need a proper evening gown for that, and then there's the charity cricket match and the strawberry tea afterwards. The bad news, though, is that Luke has three very important court cases pending so he could be called away at short notice. And of course with the baby due soon I shan't be able to do as much as I would have liked. However, once he or she arrives, you and I are going to do some serious fashion shopping, I'm so tired of maternity clothes.'

'Mmm…' Sam had enthused. 'I've read that Milan is *the* place to shop right now, the prices are really keen and you know how I love those Italian designers.'

'Mmm… Which reminds me, don't forget to bring some clam diggers, will you, and some jeans. They just don't do them over here like they do back home. Oh, and dungarees for Francesca and shirts for Luke and for James…'

'How is James?' Samantha had asked her twin coyly.

'He's fine and he's certainly looking forward to seeing you,' Bobbie had taunted her.

Samantha had laughed back. Bobbie had taunted her mercilessly at the time of her own wedding that James had fallen for her, but then Samantha had simply thought

of him as a very nice soon-to-be in-law and member of
the large Crighton clan.

Now, though, things were a little different.

Milan wasn't the only city to boast fine designer shops
and *she* had paid an extended visit to Boston prior to
doing her packing. The resultant purchases were all designed to underscore the fact that being tall did not in *any*
way mean that was not wholly and completely a woman.
A satisfied smile curled Samantha's mouth as she contemplated the effect of her new purchases on her intended
victim. James, she knew instinctively, was the kind of
man who preferred to see a woman dressed like a woman.

Her smile was replaced by a small frown as she studied
her closed suitcase. Closed it might be, but it still had to
be gotten downstairs and there was no point in calling the
man who helped with the garden to assist her. Hyram was
a honey, but he was close on seventy and there was no
way he could lift her case.

Nope... There *were* occasions when being tall and
healthily muscled were an advantage—and this, she decided, was one of them.

She negotiated the suitcase to the top of the stairs so
that she could leave it in the lobby ready for her early
morning flight and had just paused to take a rest, muttering complainingly at the overstuffed case as she did so.
Her face felt hot and flushed and the exertion had made
her hair cling in silky strands to the nape of her neck and
her flushed cheeks. Turning her back towards the stairs,
she eyed the suitcase.

'It's not just my clothes,' she told it sternly. 'It's that
sister of mine and...'

'What the...'

The unexpected sound of Liam's voice on the stairs
behind her caused Samantha to jump and turn round, for-

getting that she had momentarily balanced the case precariously on one of the stairs whilst she leaned against it to hold it in position.

The result was inevitable.

The suitcase, disobligingly ignoring her wailed protest, slid heavily down the stairs, past Liam, bouncing on the half landing before coming to a halt against a solid wooden chest where the combined effect of its speedy fall and its heavy weight caused the clasps to burst open and the contents of the case to tumble out all over the stairs.

'Oh, there now, see what you've done,' Samantha accused Liam angrily. 'If you hadn't crept up on me like that...'

'I rather think, more to the point, *you* shouldn't have overpacked the thing in the first place,' Liam corrected her dryly, turning his back on her as he headed down the stairs, hunkering down on the half landing as he proceeded to gather up the case's disgorged garments.

It was, as Samantha later seethed to herself in the privacy of her bedroom, revoltingly unfair of fate to have decreed that the stuff which had fallen out of her case wasn't the sturdy, sensible jeans she had bought for her sister, nor the dungarees for Francesca, her niece, nor even the shirts requested by her brothers-in-law, but instead, the frivolous bits of silky satin and lace items of underwear *she* had recklessly bought for herself on her shopping spree in Boston.

Creamy satin lace-trimmed bras with the kind of boning that meant that the kind of things they did for a woman's figure were strictly seriously flirtatious. And, even worse, there on the carpet beside them were the ridiculously unfunctional French knickers that had helped swallow up a large portion of her pay cheque. Add to that the equally provocative garter belt and the silk stockings and combine them with the incredulous disdain with which Liam was looking from her scarlet face to the fragile pieces of feminine lingerie he was holding in his hands and it was no wonder that she was feeling uncomfortably hot and embarrassed, Samantha reflected.

'I guess you aren't planning to do much sport in Cheshire,' Liam commented laconically. 'Or—' his eyebrows shot up as he gave her a very thorough look '—perhaps I'm wrong...' He continued silkily, 'Thinking of going hunting are you, Sam? If so...'

'They aren't mine, they're a present for Bobbie,' Samantha lied feverishly, hurrying down the stairs to snatch them away from him.

'Mmm.... Well, if you'll take my advice...as a man...something a little simpler and less structured would serve your purpose much better. These,' he told her with a contemptuous look at the boned demi bra he was holding, 'might be exciting for boys, but men...real men, prefer something a little more subtle and a lot more tactile... A sexy slither of silk and satin with tiny shoestring straps, something silky and fluid that drapes itself softly over a woman's curves, hinting at them rather than... There's nothing quite so sexy as that little hint of cleavage you get when a woman's strap slips down off her shoulder...'

'Well, thank you *very* much for your advice,' Samantha snapped furiously at him. 'But when I want *your* opinion on what a man finds sexy, Liam, you can be sure I'll ask you for it. And anyway—' She stopped abruptly.

'Anyway what?' Liam asked her mildly as he bent down again to retrieve a pretty silk wrap which was lying under the suitcase.

Samantha glared at him.

How could she tell him that when you were a woman with breasts as generously rounded and full as hers were, the type of silky clingy unstructured top *he* was describing was quite simply a "no-no" unless you wanted to stop all the traffic on the freeway.

'This isn't for Bobbie,' he told her positively as he handed her the wrap.

'What makes you say that?' Samantha demanded.

'It's not her colour,' he told her simply. 'Her skin is paler than yours and her eyes lighter. *This* is your colour, but coffee or caramel would suit you even better.'

'Thank you *so* much,' Samantha gritted acidly as she snatched the wrap from him.

As she bent to try to stuff her possessions back into her suitcase, Liam knelt down beside her.

'You need another case,' he told her calmly. 'This one, *if* you get it as far as the airport, will probably break the baggage conveyor belt. That's if it doesn't burst open again first.

'You're wrong, by the way,' he added mystifyingly as Samantha tried to ignore the reality of what he was telling her.

'It isn't only women with tiny breasts who can go bra-less. You've got far too many hang-ups about your body, Samantha, do you know that?'

'Is that a fact? Well. I'll thank you to keep your opinions on my hang-ups and my...my breasts...to yourself *if* you don't mind,' Samantha gritted hot-faced at him, wondering how he had followed her embarrassed train of thought.

'Of course, when it comes to bouncing around the tennis court, I agree that a woman needs a good sports bra,' Liam was continuing as if she hadn't spoken.

Samantha shot him a wary look. *She* played tennis in the residence's court most mornings with her father and she *always* wore a sports bra—so what was Liam implying?

'Look, why don't *I* carry this back to your room for you so that you can repack it in two cases,' Liam was offering.

To Samantha's chagrin, as he picked up the case she could see that he was able to carry it far more easily than she herself had been able to do—carrying it not downstairs where she had intended to take it, she recognised, but back in the direction she had just come—to her bedroom.

As he elbowed open the door and dumped the heavy case on the floor, Samantha followed Liam into her room.

'I *was* taking that downstairs...' she began to upbraid him and then stopped abruptly.

Standing with his feet apart and his hands on his hips, Liam wasn't watching her but instead was focusing on the pretty upholstered chair beside the window.

The chair—an antique—had been a gift from her grandmother, a pretty early Victorian rocker which Samantha had had recaned and for which she had made her own hand-stitched sampler cushions. But it wasn't the chair or the cushions which were holding Liam's attention— Samantha knew that and she knew too exactly what he was looking at.

'Mom made me keep him,' she began defensively, pushing past Liam and rushing over to the chair, protectively picking up the battered and slightly threadbare teddy bear who was seated on it.

'She says it reminds her of when we were little. It was her bear before us and then Tom had him, too, and... Oh, you don't understand,' she breathed crossly. 'You're too unemotional. Too cold...'

'You should run for government office yourself,' Liam

told her sardonically. 'With your mind-reading talent
you'd be a wow.'

'Mind-reading,' Samantha breathed heavily. 'Ol
you...'

'For your information I am *neither* unemotional *nor*
cold and as for Wilfred...' Ignoring Samantha he walked
up to her and deftly took the bear from her unresisting
grasp.

'I had one very like him when I was young. He came
originally from Ireland with my grandfather. He was just
a boy then...'

Samantha's eyes widened. Liam rarely talked about his
family—at least not to her. She knew he had no brothers
or sisters and that his grandparents, immigrants from
Ireland, had built up a very successful haulage business
which Liam's father had continued to run and expand until
his death from a heart attack whilst Liam was at college.

Liam had sold the business—very profitably—with his
mother's approval. From a very young age he had known
that he wanted to enter politics and both his parents and
his grandparents when they had been alive, had fully supported him in this ambition, but it was from her mother
that Samantha had gleaned these facts about Liam's background, not from Liam himself.

'Why does he never talk to me...treat me as an adult?'
she had once railed at her mother when Liam had point-
edly ignored some questions she had been asking him
about his grandparents. She had been at college at the time
and working on an essay about the difficulties experienced
by the country's immigrants in the earlier part of the cen-
tury and she had hoped to gain some first-hand knowledge
and insights into the subject from Liam's memories of his
grandparents.

'He's a very proud man, sweetheart,' her father had
responded, hearing her exasperated question. 'I guess he

kinda feels that he doesn't want his folks looked down on or...'

'Looked down on... Why should *I* do that?' Samantha had interrupted him indignantly.

'Well, Liam is very conscious of the fact that his grandparents came to this country with very little in the way of material possessions, just what they could carry with them in fact, whilst...'

'He thinks that *I'd* look down on him because your family arrived with Cabots and Adamses and all those other "first families" on the *Mayflower* who went on to form the backbone of North American early politics, wealth and society,' Samantha had protested hotly. 'Is that what he really thinks of me?'

'Sweetheart, sweetheart,' her father had protested gently. 'I'm sure that Liam thinks no such thing. It's just that he's as reluctant to have his family background put under the public microscope as your mother would be hers. Not out of any sense of shame—quite the reverse—but out of a very natural desire to protect those he loves.'

'But Gran is still alive whilst Liam's grandparents are dead,' Samantha had objected.

'The principle is still the same,' her father had pointed out gently.

Now, some impulse she couldn't name made Samantha ask Liam softly, 'Do you still have it...the bear...?'

His austere features suddenly broke into an almost boyish grin and for one breath-stopping moment Samantha actually felt as though something or someone was physically jerking her heartstrings. Impossible, of course, hearts didn't have strings and if hers had then there was no way that one Liam Connolly could possibly have jerked them. No, it was just the mental image she had had of him as a small boy listening solemnly to his grandfather whilst he related to him tales of his own Irish upbringing.

'Yes.'

'You'll be able to keep it for your children and tel
them the stories your grandparents told you,' Samanth
told him impulsively.

Immediately his features changed and became form
dably harsh.

'Don't you jump on the bandwagon,' he told her grit
tily. 'Everyone seems determined to marry me off. I'v
even had Lee Calder giving interviews stating that a sin
gle, childless Governor won't understand the needs of th
state's parents. My God, when I *think* of the way he'
been trying to cut down on our education.'

Lee Calder was Liam's closest contender for the gov
ernorship, a radical right-winger whose views Samantha'
father found totally unsympathetic. Lee was an over
weight, balding man in his mid-forties, twice married wit
five children who he had overdisciplined and controlle
to such an extent that the eldest, a boy, was rumoured tc
have shown his unhappiness by stealing money from hi:
parents and trashing the family home with a group o
friends one summer when the family were on vacation
without him.

No matter what her *personal* opinion of Liam might be,
Samantha knew that her father was quite right when he
said that Liam would make an excellent Governor. Highly
principled, firm, a natural leader, the state would flourish
with Liam at its helm.

Lee Calder on the other hand, despite cleverly manag
ing to package himself as a devoted family man and
churchgoer, had a string of shady dealings behind him—
nothing that could be proved, but there was something
about the man. Samantha vividly remembered the occa
sion at an official function when he had grabbed hold of
her and tried to kiss her.

Fortunately she had been able to push him away but

not before she had seen the decidedly nasty glint in his eyes as she rejected him.

She had been all of seventeen at the time and as she recalled his second wife had been pregnant with their first child.

'Don't accuse *me* of trying to marry you off,' she challenged Liam now.

'No. By the looks of what you've got in that case you're more interested in changing your own single status,' Liam agreed derisively.

'I've *told* you, *those* are for Bobbie,' Samantha insisted.

'And I've told you if *you* really want to catch yourself a man, the best way to do it is by...' He stopped when he saw her frown, then continued. 'You know that I'm driving you to the airport in the morning, don't you?'

'Yes,' Samantha agreed on a small sigh. She had a very early start and had been quite prepared to order a cab but her father could be an old-fashioned parent in some ways.

'No, sweetheart, you know what you're like for getting yourself anyplace on time.'

'Dad,' Samantha had protested, 'that was years ago...and an accident...just because I once missed a plane doesn't mean...'

'Liam's driving you,' her father had announced, and Samantha had known better than to argue with him. 'As it happens, he's picking someone up, as well.'

'Someone... Who?' Samantha had asked her father curiously.

'Someone from Washington. I want him to take her on board as his campaign PR, she's very good.'

'She?' Samantha had raised her eyebrows, her voice sharpening slightly. 'You wouldn't be doing a little matchmaking would you, Dad?'

'Give your sister our love, remember,' he had answered her obliquely, 'and tell her we can't wait to see them all....'

CHAPTER THREE

SAMANTHA checked a sleepy yawn as she ruffled her fingers through her still-damp curly crop. Despite the invigorating shower she had just taken her body was protestingly aware that it was only just gone three in the morning.

Still, she could sleep during the flight, she promised herself as she slicked a soft peachy-pink lipstick across her mouth and grimaced at her refection.

Not bad for a woman who'd slipped over thirty. Her skin was still as clear and fresh-looking as it had been ten years ago and even if there was now a deeper maturity and wisdom in her eyes than any twenty-year-old could have, a person was going to have to stand pretty close to her to see it.

James was in his mid-thirties but he had that boyish look about him that a few Englishmen have. Although equally as tall and strongly built as his elder brother Luke and just as stunningly handsome, James had about him a certain sweetness of nature which more austere men like his brother, and to some extent Liam, too, lacked. James was, in short, an absolute honey. He would be very easy to love, a wonderful husband and father...and an equally wonderful lover? The kind of lover she knew instinctively a man like *Liam* would be.

Samantha put down her lipstick and frowned. Now what on earth had put *that* thought into her head?

Liam as a lover...! Her lover? No way at all!

She glanced at her watch. Time she was downstairs.

Liam would be picking her up in five minutes and he was very hot on good timekeeping.

Even though she had said her goodbyes to her parents the previous evening, she wasn't totally surprised to have them rush downstairs minutes before she left to hug and kiss her and reiterate their messages of love to her twin as well as the rest of the Crightons.

'Don't forget that your grandparents should be arriving in Haslewich during the time you are there,' Samantha's mother reminded her.

'How could I forget anything involving Grandma Ruth?' Samantha teased her mother.

Ruth Crighton, as she had been before her late marriage to Sarah Jane's father, was affectionately known as Aunt Ruth to virtually all of the Crighton family and so had become Grandma Ruth to Bobbie, Samantha and their younger brother.

Blissfully married at last to the American soldier she had first met during the Second World War, Ruth divided her time together with her husband between Haslewich and Grant's beautiful American house.

'Better not keep Liam waiting,' her father counselled as they all heard the knock on the door.

She went to let him in and he thanked her before going over to her mother to give her a very easy and natural almost filially warm hug. Samantha acknowledged grudgingly that there was no way she could ever fault Liam's behaviour towards her parents. He might deliberately rub *her* up the wrong way, inciting her to open rebellion and sometimes even outright war, but no one could have faked the look of very real warmth and affection he was giving her folks.

'I see you took my advice about the suitcases,' was his

only comment to her once they were inside his car and he had loaded her two cases into its trunk.

Samantha scowled at him.

'My decisions to repack had nothing to do with you,' she told him loftily and a mite untruthfully. 'Mom wanted me to take some extra gifts over for the family.'

The derisory look Liam was giving her silenced her.

'Dad said you were picking up a Washington PR expert from the airport,' she commented, deliberately changing the subject.

'Mmm...'

'You surprise me, Liam,' she told him. 'I thought you were far too confident to feel you needed any image polishing or manipulating.'

'*I* don't,' Liam assured her, 'but some of your father's supporters are concerned that Lee Calder could be planning to market himself as the family's champion and they want to start up a damage limitation exercise.'

'By what, marrying you off to this PR woman?' Samantha asked flippantly before adding, 'Wouldn't it be simpler just to marry your current date...whoever she is...'

'There *is* no current date,' Liam told her. 'And to be frank, Samantha, I'm getting rather tired of this image you keep trying to push of me as some kind of serial ladykiller. For your information—' He broke off, cursing as a truck suddenly swerved out of a side street in front of them.

Samantha was far too glad of the diversion to reintroduce the same topic of conversation once the truck had gone. Much as she enjoyed baiting Liam, she also knew when it was wise to back off a little.

'I could say much the same thing to you, you know,' Liam murmured, turning his head to look directly at her as she turned towards him, warily waiting for what he was going to say.

'If you're as keen to prove to your colleagues as you said that you are woman enough to be a mother, then there are far easier ways of doing so than going looking in England for a man to father your child.'

'What are you suggesting—artificial insemination. No way!' Angrily Samantha turned away from him, staring in silence out of the car window.

Liam was a good driver and long before they had crossed the state line Samantha had dropped off to sleep, her body angled towards Liam's, one hand resting under her face.

After he'd safely overtaken a truck, Liam turned his head to look at her. She had to be one of the most breathtakingly stunning women he had ever seen. Her sister Bobbie was beautiful but where Bobbie exuded an air of relaxed self-control, Samantha was a bundle of quicksilver fieriness, impulsive, impatient, almost too sensitive for her own good at times, proud and...

Liam cursed under his breath. As *he* knew all too well, there were almost no lengths Samantha would not go to to prove her point if someone hurt her pride. And he knew better than most, having watched both girls grow up, that despite all the positive influences they had received from their parents and family, both of them, but especially Samantha, were privately a little sensitive about their height.

Liam could remember overhearing a much younger Samantha telling her mother in a low voice choked with tears, 'Mom, the other girls at school say that I should have been a boy because I'm so big...but I'm not a boy, I'm a girl and...'

'They're just jealous of you, darling,' her mother had

reassured her quickly. 'You are indeed a girl, a very beautiful, clever and lovable girl, a very feminine girl,' she had reinforced, and Liam had watched as Sarah Jane had very cleverly and with maternal love and concern, made sure that her daughters learned how to focus on the very feminine aspects of their personalities, to hold their heads up with pride and grace.

They *were* tall, and as a teenager Samantha especially had gone through a phase when she had been all gangly limbs, a little lanky and perhaps almost boyish, but that had been as a teenager. Now she was all woman... Oh, yes...now she was very definitely all woman!

Waking up beside him, Samantha wondered what had caused that sudden burst of fire to ignite the darkness of Liam's eyes. Whatever it was, whoever it was... Was it a whoever rather than a whatever? Samantha suddenly wondered. The new PR woman perhaps? She gave a small, quick, sharp intake of breath. Liam might be prepared to bow to the fears of the more conservative lobby and do the conventional thing, marry in order to improve his public appeal, but there was no power on earth that could ever force her to do the same thing. Her principles, her need of her own self-respect, were far too strong, but Liam of course, was far too pragmatic to understand such a sensitive point of view. Cousin James in Chester was very sensitive. She had noticed that in him the moment they had met, and had been touched and warmed by it and by his concern for her.

James.

She was *already* beginning to feel a very definite tingle of excitement at the thought of seeing him again. The Crighton men made wonderful fathers, even the family's erstwhile outcast Max had totally and unexpectedly shown that he possessed the loving Crighton gene when it came to parenting.

'He seems more thrilled about this new baby they're expecting than Maddy is,' Bobbie had confided to her sister when she had passed on to her the news that Max's wife Maddy was pregnant with their third child.

'A reconciliation baby,' Samantha had commented. 'Well, I hope it works—for the new baby's sake.'

'Mmm... I can't get over how their relationship has turned around,' Bobbie had continued. 'Max seems to have completely given up his old ways. He's based himself in Chester now and he and Luke have developed a rapport I would have thought completely impossible at one time.

'It's Maddy who's changed the most, though. I thought that with Max back at home, recovered from the vicious attack he suffered in Jamaica and so completely repentant and determined to make their marriage work that Maddy would have reverted to her previous role of full-time wife and mother—after all, it's no sinecure, not when you think of what running a house like Queensmead entails, and the fact that she's also got Ben living with them.

'I know she thinks the world of him and him of her, and of course Max has always been his favourite grandchild, but that doesn't alter the fact that he can be very irascible and that he holds very strong and old-fashioned views. But no, instead, she's not only kept on the work she was doing for Grandma Ruth's mother and children charity, but she's actually got even *more* involved. Luke told me the other day that Max had admitted that he sometimes felt as though he needed to make an appointment in order to get Maddy's undivided attention these days.'

'Mmm...well I certainly noticed how much she's blossomed the last time I was over,' Samantha had agreed.

Previously she had found that Maddy, with her self-effacing timid ways, although sweet-natured and gentle, wasn't someone she felt particularly drawn to, but on her last visit she had been not just amazed and intrigued by the change in her, but she had also discovered how interesting and entertaining Maddy was to talk with.

'She certainly has. Her latest thing is that she's instituted a bi-monthly women's night out when we all get together and leave the men in charge of the babes. We all host the event in turn and it's amazing the different things everyone comes up with. It's my turn next and I was wondering if we could bribe the men into extending their child-minding so that we might have a weekend in New York.'

Recalling their conversation now, Sam remembered, too, how she had felt just that little bit envious of her sister's almost idyllic lifestyle. Her own friends, the girls she had grown up with and then met at college, were scattered all over the States and beyond them, some married, some not, and whilst they all kept in sporadic touch there was not the close-knit sense of community, of family, between them that Bobbie had become so much a part of in her life in England.

Samantha knew enough of small close-knit communities from her childhood in New England to be aware that sometimes they could be restrictive and even stultifying but... But the pluses were greater than the minuses in the balance sheet of life, at least in her opinion, and the teasing affectionate friendships which she had witnessed existing between her twin and the other members of the Crighton clan were something she couldn't help contrasting with her own sense of alienation and separateness from her own work colleagues.

They were approaching the airport now, the freeway

increasingly busy. What was she like, Liam's new PR? Intelligent? Sparky? Glamorous? All of those and very probably a whole lot more, Samantha decided. Her father had certainly sounded impressed by her.

Was that why she was experiencing these unfamiliar little tickles of antipathy and this disobliging sense of not wanting to like the other woman? Samantha wondered ruefully.

Liam had parked the car and was opening his door.

'I'll get you a trolley,' he was informing her.

'For goodness' sake, Liam,' she snapped. 'Stop smothering me. I'm perfectly capable of getting my own trolley. I'm a big girl, remember...'

'Maybe, but I'm an old-fashioned man,' he reminded her almost tersely. 'Wait here...'

'Wait here!' Samantha opened her mouth to snap angrily that she would do no such thing but it was too late, he was already striding determinedly to where the baggage carts were stacked.

Typically she discovered when he returned with one, unlike her he had managed to find one that wheeled smoothly and easily.

'Liam,' she protested fiercely when he insisted on pushing it for her.

'What *is* it with you?' he demanded grittily. 'You know your trouble, don't you, Samantha?' He answered his own question without allowing her any time to make her own response. 'You're afraid of being a woman. You're afraid of...'

'I'm no such thing,' Samantha interrupted him furiously. 'I...'

'Yes, you are,' Liam taunted her. 'Look at the way you even prefer to be called Sam instead of Samantha.'

'That's not because…it's just easier for people to say…quicker…'

Liam's eyebrows lifted.

'Quicker maybe, but nowhere near as sexy.'

'Sexy!' She glared at him.

'Mmm… Samantha…' He said her name slowly, drawing out each syllable. 'Samantha is a woman's name and like a woman should be lingered over and enjoyed the way a man…'

'Thanks for the psychoanalysis,' Samantha snapped fiercely, 'but I've got a plane to catch, remember, Liam? So, if you want to do some lingering I suggest you wait until you've picked up your new PR. *She* might be more impressed than…'

'See, you're doing it now,' Liam stopped her softly. 'What is it you're really afraid of, Samantha…? I'll take a guess that it isn't not being enough of a woman…it's being *too* much of one.'

Samantha stared at him, for once completely lost for words. His soft-voiced comment had struck unnervingly close to home, too close… To have someone, *anyone*, see so deeply and intimately into her most private self was a disturbing enough act on its own, but when that someone was *Liam*, a man who she had dismissed as someone too prosaic…too practical…too unemotional to…

'I need to check in,' she told him, making a grab for the trolley only too relieved to have an excuse for both changing the subject and escaping his presence and her own thoughts.

'Mmm…'

Instead of relinquishing the trolley handle Liam kept hold of it so that her hands were resting close to the warmth of his and then, before she could guess what he intended to do, Liam moved with surprising swiftness, covering her hands with his own and keeping her captive, his head bending over hers in the same half beat of time that she lifted her face towards him in irritable surprise.

'Li—,' she began but got no further than the first syllable of his name before his mouth was covering hers.

He had only kissed her very occasionally before, brief non-sexual courtesy kisses on her cheek and so she was completely unprepared for the reaction the hard determined pressure of his mouth evoked from her now.

Her pulse gave an unexpected shock-cum-thrill little flutter that left her feeling breathless and light-headed. Or was it the increasingly firm pressure of Liam's mouth that was doing that? An unexpectedly delicious and temptingly enjoyable firm pressure, the kind of firm pressure that made her sigh softly and lean responsively into him, her own lips starting to part on what just might have been a give-away small sound of heady pleasure.

It was, of course, the bright lights of the airport that were making her close her eyes and then open them slowly again to focus hazily and wonderingly on the deep smouldering depths of Liam's—of course it was. Languorously, Samantha felt her lips soften against his… Mmm…but it was such a lovely kiss, such a sensuous, nerve-skittering, heart-thrillingly sexy kiss that she would have to have been made of stone to resist it.

But…

Abruptly she stiffened, realising just where her thoughts were heading, and firmly she pushed him away.

'Thank you, Liam,' she told him sweetly. 'That was very nice but shouldn't you be saving it for someone more…appreciative…'

His eyebrows rose as he released her.

'Much *more* appreciation and they'd have been hauling us up for indecency,' Liam drawled back.

'Indecency…' Samantha shot him a fiercely indignant look, preparing to do battle, and then stopped, her face flushing as she saw the brief, oh so wryly explicit look he was giving her body.

There was no need of course for *her* to look down at her T-shirt-clad breasts to see just how tautly erect her nipples now were. *She* could feel it…them.

'That's just—' she began defensively.

Liam stopped her, shaking his head as he told her dryly, 'You don't need to tell *me* what it is, hon,' he drawled. 'In fact—'

'They'll be calling my flight,' Samantha told him, desperate to escape.

She knew her face must be flushed because her body felt hot. Her mind was burning with questions and her instinctive need was simply to escape just as fast as she could, to avoid any kind of confrontation. *Not* with Liam, no, it was *herself* she didn't feel able to confront, her *own* inexplicable behaviour and reactions. Grabbing hold of the trolley, she started to walk away from Liam as quickly as she could, refusing to give in to the temptation to turn round and see what he was doing—how he was looking.

The girl at the check-in desk gave her a calmly professional smile as she checked her travel documents and indicated that Samantha was to put her luggage on the conveyor.

Samantha could feel a prickling sensation running jarringly up and down her spine. She just *knew* that Liam was still there watching her. Unable to stop herself, she turned round, her mouth opening in a small O of disbelief when she couldn't see him. He had gone already. Aggrieved she double-checked the area where she had left him, muttering beneath her breath as she did so, 'Well, thanks very much...'

It was typical of him, of course, to behave in such an outrageously high-handed manner and then simply walk away without any explanation. No doubt if she had asked him for one he would have responded with something unflattering.

The check-in girl was indicating that she was to go through to the departure area. Briefly Samantha hesitated but there was still no sign of Liam. No doubt he was far more interested in meeting this new PR person than he was in seeing *her* off.

A little forlornly Samantha went through into the departure lounge.

From his vantage point, well away from the busy main concourse, Liam watched as Samantha set off on her journey. Kissing her like that had been a mistake and mistakes were something that Liam did not normally allow himself to make. It wasn't good policy for an ambitious young politician. Ambitious...young... Liam gave a semi self-derisory little smile.

Young he most certainly no longer was—and as for ambitious? Recently he had become increasingly aware that he had absorbed much more from working with Samantha's father than the mere mechanics, the bare bones of what the governorship of their small state actually involved.

Stephen Miller was a true philanthropist. Someone who genuinely wanted to improve the lot of his fellow men, to raise their expectations of life and their belief in themselves in ways both temporal and secular. A rapport had developed between them which had touched upon the sensitive and idealistic side of Liam's nature, the Celtic inheritance which believed so strongly in the right of the human race to stand proud and free.

His ambitions now no longer centred on Washington or the personal goal of high office. In stepping into Stephen Miller's shoes, he would be granted a unique opportunity to build on foundations so secure and true that ultimately they could support a society as near to perfection as man with his inherently flawed nature could ever get. Their health care programme, their record for supporting the more needy, especially the elderly, was already being lauded as a model on which other states should base their own programmes.

Their high school drop-out rate was decreasing every year and one of Liam's own goals would be to find a means of motivating the less intellectually gifted and of giving them both a sense of self-worth and the respect of others.

Liam didn't believe in deluding himself. Getting the governorship was but the first very small step in what was going to be a long, testing and arduous journey. There was no space in his life either now or in the foreseeable future for...complications.

Other people might claim that he needed a wife but the kind of wife he had in mind, as he knew very well, the kind of *marriage* he had in mind, was a carefully organised and businesslike political partnership, a marriage where it was automatically acknowledged that his work would come first.

The cool analytical controlled side of his nature agreed with this, the idealistic, passionate Celtic side did not.

He saw the tiny frown, the quickly hidden forlorn look Samantha gave the empty space where he had been standing before turning and walking away.

He could still vividly remember the impact she had had

on him the first time he had seen her. A teenager she might have been, but her burgeoning womanhood had still been there for those with the eyes to see it. She might have been shy and a little awkward, blushingly self-conscious about the crush she had had on him, but he had been all too well aware of the powerful strength of the womanly passion she would ultimately own.

Pride and passion—they were a dangerous combination in any woman, but most especially in one like Samantha who also had such a strong maternal yearning.

He had seen the look in her eyes as she held other women's babies, when she played with her twin's little girl. If her pride and her idealism had been less he suspected that she might, long ago, have settled for a mundane marriage to a man who allowed her to control their relationship whilst she gave the full passion of her love to their children, but Samantha wasn't like that. There was no way she could ever allow herself to accept second-best. But now the cruel gibes of her work colleagues had galvanised her into action and she was determined to prove him and them wrong.

Liam frowned. It was time for him to go and meet the Washington flight. Samantha had been more on the mark than she knew with her slightly waspish comments about Toni Davis. Ostensibly she was quite simply joining his campaign in a PR capacity, but Liam was no fool. He knew perfectly well that one of the reasons her name had been put forward was because she would make a perfect political wife. Subtle, discreet, content to remain in the background and to exercise her ambitions via her husband, Toni Davis was the complete antithesis to Samantha who had *never* learned to fully control her emotions and realise that the best way to do battle for her beliefs was not always the most upfront and open way.

He could hear the Washington flight being announced. As he lifted his arm to look at his watch Liam recognised that the scent wafting from his jacket was Samantha's.

CHAPTER FOUR

'SAM...over here....'

Samantha checked and then waved frantically, her face breaking into a wide beaming smile as she caught sight of Bobbie's brother-in-law and her cousin, James Crighton, waiting for her on the other side of the airport arrivals barrier.

'James, what a lovely surprise,' she cried, hugging him enthusiastically. More than one person stopped to admire the attractive picture they made. James, tall, dark and boyishly good-looking, and Samantha, almost equally as tall and stunningly eye-catching with her golden-blonde hair, their arms wrapped around one another as they kissed with genuine affection.

'Mmm...' James murmured appreciatively, a teasing glint in his eyes as Samantha started to disengage herself. 'That was nice...'

'*Very* nice,' Samantha agreed with laughing playfulness, offering him saucily, 'Want another...'

Laughter gurgled in her throat at the look that James was giving her. They had always gotten on well together but where she was all quicksilver reactions and emotions, James was far more laid back and calm which she found blissfully soothing.

'People are watching,' James warned her as his lips touched hers.

'Who cares,' Sam returned recklessly, but he still released her, Samantha noticed. Now Liam would not only

56

have mocked *her* he would also have deliberately and arrogantly ignored everybody else.

Liam! Why on earth was she thinking about him now? It should be James she was concentrating on. Beneath her lashes she flicked him a considering look. It was easy to dismiss and overlook the attractiveness of James's smile, the sheer niceness of him, in favour of the spectacularly smouldering sexuality of his cousin Saul, the austere, exciting sensuality of his brother Luke, the sledgehammer onslaught of the outrageous physical appeal of his other cousin Max, but James, in his own way was every bit as special and sexy as the other Crighton men, even if he came across as being rather more gentle, a little less macho and hormonally charged.

Personally *she* preferred James to the others. His presence was so relaxing and soothing. She loved the calming effect he had on her, so very different from the hostile aggression Liam so often aroused in her. James would make a wonderful father. She could see him now...

'Bobbie said to apologise for not being able to meet you herself. Francesca's had a bit of a chesty cough and she didn't want to leave her.'

'Oh, poor little girl,' Samantha instantly sympathised. 'How is she...? Is she...?'

'It's nothing too serious,' James assured her. 'It's just that she's been a bit fretful.'

'Well, it's very kind of you to make time to meet me,' Samantha thanked him. 'The last time I spoke to Bobbie she mentioned how busy both you and Luke are.'

'Mmm... Well thankfully, since Max joined the chambers the pressure has eased off a little, or at least it was doing but, well I shouldn't complain about the fact that we seem to be attracting more briefs than ever. Aarlston-Becker have been placing a considerable amount of work our way via Saul and increasingly I seem to be finding that I'm spending more and more of my time in the Hague involved in lengthy international cases.'

Aarlston-Becker was the multi-national concern with offices in Haslewich, and Saul Crighton, a member of the Haslewich side of the Crighton family through his father Hugh, her own grandmother Ruth's half-brother, headed the legal team and so it was quite natural that when he needed the expert opinion of a barrister that he should apply to his own family for it.

'Dad was complaining only the other day about how much the legal profession has changed,' James continued. 'Historically, of course, barristers did have specific and special areas of expertise, now these areas have become much more individually defined. We've even been talking about taking on a new member of Chambers due to the amount of medical compensation cases we've been getting.'

'Pity I'm not qualified in that field myself,' Samantha told him doe-eyed.

'*You're* looking for a career move?' James asked her interestedly.

'Sort of,' Samantha responded tongue-in-cheek, her eyes dancing with amusement as she wondered what he would say if she were to tell him in just exactly *what* direction she was envisaging her career moving and why.

'Would you mind if we called on my parents on the way back?' James was asking her as he guided her towards his waiting car.

'No, not at all,' Samantha responded promptly.

She had already met James' parents and the rest of his family on several occasions and had got on well with them.

She knew from Bobbie that they had just moved to a

ground-floor apartment in a recently renovated large Victorian house on the banks of the Dee.

'Henry loves it,' Bobbie had told Samantha, referring to her father-in-law. 'He spent hours wrangling with the builders over the quality of workmanship and Pat says that taking charge of the owners association has given him a new lease of life.

'Luke complains that he can see a lot of his father's stubbornness in Francesca...'

'His *father's* stubbornness,' Samantha had repeated drolly, whilst Bobbie had laughed ruefully.

'Okay, okay, I know, I have my fair share of that particular vice, no need to rub it in. Still, a little toughness won't do Fran any harm, not if she's going to follow family tradition and go into the law.'

'Fran! No way,' Samantha had told her twin robustly. 'She's going to be running the country at the very least.'

The Cheshire countryside in sunshine had to be one of the prettiest sights there was, Samantha reflected happily as she sat next to James in comfortable silence as he drove them towards Chester.

In the distance beyond the fertile neatly checkered fields lay the blue haze of the Welsh mountains. No wonder in centuries gone by there had been so much feuding over the Welsh border. No wonder warring English kings had needed to build so many strong castles to protect their rich domain.

It was a humbling thought to remember that the Romans had farmed these lands and mined the rich vein of salt from which the town of Haslewich had got its wealth and its name.

Now the salt was no longer mined and the modern legacy that industry had left was one of flooded salt works and dangerously unstable buildings.

As though he had read her mind James commented conversationally, 'We've got an interesting case at the moment. A local farmer is trying to sue Aarlston-Becker because he claims the weight of the company's headquarters is causing subsidence on his land.'

'Oh, and is it?' Samantha asked him interestedly.

'Hard to say, but certainly it's a topic which arouses an awful lot of emotions. It's the classic story of the old guard being suspicious of the new incomers. The case had been given a lot of local publicity. Aarlston has an image to maintain of a socially aware and ecologically sound organisation so, in the end, to protect that image they may have to opt for a one-off payment to the farmer. His land is over a mile away but he maintains that because of the interlinking network of mines and tunnels beneath the ground, the weight of the Aarlston building is being reflected in land subsidence some distance away.'

'Mmm...sounds like a try-on to me,' Samantha pronounced.

'Mmm...indeed,' James conceded, returning the laughing smile Samantha was giving him, his gaze lingering for just a shade longer than was merely cousinly on her face.

A small sensation of happy warmth curled up through Samantha's body. Coming to England had quite definitely been the right decision. What she would give to have Cliff witness that look she had just seen in James' eyes.

They would make the most beautiful babies together. Samantha gave a small contented sigh.

How thoughtful of fate to give her plans an active boost like this. Keeping her voice carefully neutral she told James, 'With her pregnancy and everything Bobbie has her hands pretty full at the moment...'

Deliberately she affected a small downcast sigh. 'I was

so looking forward to seeing a bit more of the area, too, and of catching up with the rest of the family.'

'Well, if you need an escort I'*d* be more than happy to offer my services,' James responded gallantly.

Samantha produced a slightly self-conscious look, flapping her eyelashes and exclaiming, 'Oh, James, would you...? That would be so kind, although I didn't mean...'

'It would be my pleasure,' James assured her fervently.

She really wasn't behaving very well at all, Samantha reflected a little guiltily, but it was for the very best of causes and if she hadn't sensed that James liked her...

They were just outside Chester now and Samantha could feel the excitement starting to bubble up inside her. She was so looking forward to being with Bobbie. She gave an exultant sigh and closed her eyes. What would Liam make of Chester, she wondered. He would be impossibly well informed about its long history, of course, with every fact and figure at his fingertips, and whilst *she* fantasised about the romanticism of its history, he would no doubt insist on bringing her down to earth by reminding her of the savagery and bloodshed it must have known.

Angrily Samantha opened her eyes. Liam! *Why* on earth was she thinking about *him?* Just because he had kissed her? Just because she...

'Are you okay?' James was asking her, sensing the tension, his forehead creased in concern.

'I'm fine,' Samantha assured him, but somehow it felt as though a small cloud had been cast over the exultation she had felt earlier. It was stupid of her to compare the warm, affectionate, almost brotherly touch of James' lips to the hard, pulse-dizzying possession of Liam's, and *why* was she doing it anyway? Liam's kiss hadn't meant *anything* to her.

Not cerebrally maybe, but her *body* had certainly responded to it—to *him*.

An accident; an aberration, a faulty bit of sexual programming, that was all that had been.

'You've gone quiet. Are you tired?' James asked her solicitously.

'A mite jet-lagged I guess,' Samantha agreed, gratefully seizing on the excuse he had given her for her lapse in concentration. James was so wonderfully caring and considerate.

'We're here now,' he told her as he swung his small sporty car in through a pair of high wrought-iron gates which opened automatically for them.

The builders who had renovated and converted the large Victorian house into apartments had taken great care to maintain the original facade and to provide well-secured grounds around it. An immaculate expanse of gravel swept round to the front of the building. No parking bays had been marked out on it but James informed Samantha drolly that there was a definite parking spot for each apartment and woe betide anyone who parked in the wrong place.

'I think if he could get away with it Dad would impose "on the spot" fines on unwitting miscreants parking in the wrong place,' he told her ruefully.

'It's a magnificent house,' Samantha enthused, automatically reaching for the passenger door handle of the car, but before she could swing it open James was out of the car, sprinting round to the door to open it for her.

There was always a certain formality and protocol attached to being a member of the Governor's family but Samantha couldn't remember the last time a *date* had proved so solicitous towards her.

From its elevated position on the banks of the Dee the

house overlooked the river itself and the countryside beyond it and Samantha could well appreciate why James' parents had wanted to move here.

'With none of us left at home Ma was finding the house far too large and with three storeys, each with a flight of stairs, it made sense to move to somewhere more easily manageable.'

As he spoke, James was guiding Samantha towards the main entrance to the building.

A special security card was needed to gain entrance into the inner hallway, coolly elegant in cream marble and illuminated with an enormous crystal chandelier.

'It's this way,' James told her, indicating a pair of handsome carved doors on the left and going up to them to press the bell.

Almost immediately the door was opened by James' mother. Although Patricia Crighton was a very attractive-looking woman, it was from their father that Luke and James had inherited their striking dark good looks.

'Samantha, my dear, do come in,' Patricia Crighton greeted her, kissing Samantha warmly on the cheek.

The drawing room the older woman took Samantha to was filled with the elegant antiques Samantha remembered from their previous home. There was, she noticed, a very recent photograph of her twin sister with her husband Luke and their little girl amongst the other family photographs on top of the elegant Queen Anne side table.

'Is Dad here? I've got those papers he asked me for,' James said to his mother.

'He's in his study, darling,' she responded, adding, 'Oh, and by the way, we've got a visitor.' She stopped, giving James a rather wary look, and then the drawing room door opened to admit her husband and a young woman who Samantha did not recognise.

'Rosemary, what the devil are you doing here?' she heard James demanding sharply, the antagonism so very evident in his voice and his demeanour that Samantha looked at him in surprise. Suddenly he looked and sounded so very much more like his elder brother, so very forcibly a Crighton, and it was obvious from his expression what his feelings were for the girl who had just walked into the room. What on earth had she done to make James, of all people, dislike her so much? Samantha wondered curiously.

Small and red-headed, she had a neat triangular-shaped face with high cheek-bones and huge amber-flecked golden eyes. Although she was wearing jeans and a T-shirt there was no disguising the rounded voluptuousness of her figure. Her waist was tiny, Samantha noticed, so small that she guessed a man could easily span it with his hands.

'Rosemary, my dear,' James' mother was beginning but the girl wasn't paying any attention to her, instead she was concentrating wholly and completely on James, fixing him with a fulminating look of bitter hostility.

'Oh, it's all right, Aunt Pat,' she announced with an angry toss of her head. 'Far be it from me to point out that since this isn't James' house *he* doesn't really have any right to question my presence here. Your mother has invited me to come and stay with her, James,' she added, baring her teeth in a smile that made Samantha think of an angry and dangerous little cat.

'Rosemary needed a break,' James' mother was saying palliatively. 'She's worked so hard for her finals and now that she's qualified...'

'Qualified?' James interrupted sharply. 'God help anyone who needs...who's desperate enough to need *your* medical expertise, Rosemary. Personally I'd sooner...'

'James,' his mother commanded warningly.

Two brilliant coins of hot colour were now burning in the girl's creamy pale skin and her eyes... Samantha grimaced a little as she studied their furious molten heat. Small she might be, but there was no mistaking the ferocity of her emotions.

'Rosemary has just finished her medical training and qualified as a GP,' James' mother informed Samantha gently. 'And since I'm her godmother I felt that her hard work and dedication deserved rewarding with a small treat, especially since her fiancé Tim is going to be working abroad all summer.'

As James' mother spoke Rosemary lifted her hand, showing off the diamond ring she was wearing, the look she gave James a mixture of defiance and triumph.

'You see, James,' she told him, 'not all men share your opinion of me.'

'You're engaged!' It was plain to see how shocked James was. 'What a masochist!'

'James!' Pat Crighton expostulated sharply.

Grimly James turned towards his father.

'A small treat,' James picked up on what his mother had said. 'So you've invited her to stay here for a few weeks...' His voice full of disgust.

'Here are the papers you asked me for,' he said to his father, turning his back on his mother and Rosemary.

'We must go,' he informed them all. 'Bobbie is expecting us and Samantha's beginning to feel a little jet-lagged.'

'It's probably something to do with a lack of oxygen,' Rosemary chipped in in mock sympathy, something about the acid sweetness of her voice causing Samantha to focus on her more closely. When she did so the outright hostility in the other girl's eyes startled her.

'Rosemary...' she could hear James beginning warningly, but it was becoming clear to Samantha that the redhead had as reckless a hot temper and an emotionally driven streak as her hair colour suggested because she deliberately ignored him and continued.

'It can't be easy inhabiting such a rarefied atmosphere...*or* being so tall...'

Samantha's eyes widened a little. The other girl's hostility totally perplexed her but cat fights had never been her style...even so...

'Mmm...but it does have its compensations,' she drawled in her best and most laid-back American voice, turning from the girl to James who was standing protectively by her side.

If she stood up on her toes they were almost exactly shoulder to shoulder, face to face, lips to lips.

Very deliberately Samantha looked into James' eyes and then allowed her glance to slide downward to his mouth before touching her tongue tip to her own upper lip.

'Er... I think we'd better leave,' James announced thickly.

Samantha permitted herself a languorous look of superiority in the direction of Rosemary and then checked it as she saw not just bitter fury in the girl's eyes but the hot glimmer of tears, as well.

Tears? For James? But she was wearing another man's ring. Thoughtfully Samantha said goodbye to James' parents and followed him out to the car.

'I don't know what on earth's possessed my mother to invite Rosemary to stay,' James was fuming as he started his car's engine.

'They obviously get on well together and since Rosemary is her goddaughter...'

'Rosemary is a menace...a...' James said. 'But my mother can't or won't see it.'

'She's very pretty,' Samantha offered, trying another tack.

'Pretty...' James stared at her. 'She was a red-haired brat with freckles.'

'Mmm...well, she's *still* red-haired,' Samantha agreed.

'She used to come and stay with us during the school holidays. Her parents worked abroad and she was at boarding school.'

'You didn't get on with her?' Samantha guessed.

'...and the rest,' James agreed. 'She really was the most loathsome little pest. "I'll tell Aunt Pat..."'' he mimicked and then shook his head. 'I know you must think I'm overreacting but she really used to get under my skin.'

He wasn't drawing a very attractive picture of the other girl and given her unwarranted and unprovoked malicious comment to herself, Samantha might have agreed with him but for those unexpected tears. Rosemary's feelings for James were no concern of hers, Samantha reminded herself, and since she had her own plans for James' future...and since Rosemary herself was engaged... Even so she couldn't help wishing that she hadn't seen those tears, that she hadn't for that brief pulse of time felt the other girl's distress.

'Come on then, give me all the news about the family,' Bobbie urged her twin.

They were sitting in Bobbie's comfortable kitchen, James having just left, whilst Francesca played busily around them.

'There isn't that much *to* tell that you don't already know,' Samantha protested. 'Mom and Dad can't wait to get over here to see you all...'

'Mmm…I'm hoping to persuade them to spend more time over here when Dad retires. How's Liam's campaign going, by the way?'

'Dad's convinced he'll walk it but there has been concern expressed over Liam not being married. He drove me to the airport. He was picking up a PR woman they've hired from Washington to project his image.'

'Liam married, how will *you* feel about that?' Bobbie teased her.

Samantha shot her an indignant look.

'Why should *I* care. Just because I once had a teenage crush on him…'

'Okay, okay…I was just joking,' Bobbie reassured her, but she still studied her twin a little thoughtfully.

Samantha had lost some weight and she looked strained…stressed…

'You know, Bobbie, I do envy you,' Samantha admitted abruptly.

Instinctively Bobbie looked to where Francesca was playing, knowing without it having to be put into words just what it was about her life that her twin envied.

'You're a born mother, Sam,' she told her gently, her expression suddenly changing to one of acute alarm as she demanded, 'You're not thinking of going through with that fool idea you once had of becoming pregnant via a fertilization programme…'

Samantha laughed.

'No,' she reassured her, her face sobering as she admitted, 'I don't want my kids growing up envying yours because yours have a real live daddy and mine don't.'

'So there isn't a prospective daddy anywhere on the horizon?' Bobbie probed.

Samantha looked away from her.

'Samantha!' Bobbie pounced excitedly. 'There *is* some-one...tell me... Who is it? Do I know him...? Sam...'

'Oh, no... I'm not saying anything,' Samantha told her, vehemently shaking her head.

'I'm going to phone home,' Bobbie threatened deter-minedly.

'There isn't any point, the folks don't know any more than you do...'

'So there *is* something to know then...'

'No!' Samantha denied.

There was no way she intended to let Bobbie in on her plan to marry James until she was a lot more certain of her own ground. Sure she and James got on well together but... She *could* love him, Samantha was convinced of it, and he, she was equally sure, could love her.

He would be a *perfect* father. She could see it all now. She closed her eyes blissfully, mentally imagining her own cosy homely kitchen and her own adorable children filling it. She wanted boys, she knew that already, boys with thick dark hair and solemn grey eyes... Grey eyes... Her own flew open. Now where, oh, where, had *that* idea come from? Firmly she recorrected her imagination. Her children, her *twins,* would have eyes the same colour as their father's of course. They would have James' *brown* eyes.

Having finished her game, Francesca stood up and stalked imperiously towards her.

'Did you bring me a present from my grandma in America?' she asked her.

'Francesca,' Bobbie protested warningly.

But Samantha only grinned and asked her twin dryly, 'Wonder where she gets *that* from?'

'Not from me,' Bobbie denied, but her face was pink and she knew as clearly as though she had read

Samantha's mind that her twin was remembering an incident from their own childhood when she, Bobbie, had shamingly asked much the same question of their own grandfather.

'Poor Mom was *so* mortified,' Samantha teased her.

'Not half so mortified as I was when she banished me upstairs to my room *and* I haven't forgotten that *you* were the one who told me to ask.' Bobbie said with heartfelt ruefulness.

After they had finished, still laughing, Samantha confided to her twin, 'I've bought her the cutest outfits.'

'Mmm… Well I may as well warn you that if it isn't Barbie doll pink then Francesca won't even *look* at it.'

'No… How can you doubt me?' Samantha responded, grinning at her. 'She'll *love* it.'

'Samantha…' Bobbie warned warily. 'What…'

'I've even got her the matching sparkling pink shoes and…strictly for dressing up, of course,' she assured her stern-faced twin.

'…and for you I made a special trip to Boston. I've got you the sexiest Donna Karan number you've *ever* seen. It dips right down at the back so that… Not that you'll be able to wear it until after the new baby arrives—but still that won't be long now!'

'You have…where…*show me…*' Bobbie demanded excitedly.

The pair of them were still giggling over the clothes-strewn spare room when Luke arrived home over an hour later.

'Auntie Sam brought me pink shoes,' Francesca informed him proudly.

Laughing Samantha shook her head as she kissed her brother-in-law.

'Guess what I've brought you…'

'I don't think I dare,' Luke drawled, looking past her to where his wife, all pink-cheeked and bright-eyed was holding up in front of her a dress that Luke could immediately see would cause a total uproar if she ever wore it in public. Bobbie looked like a little girl clutching on to a much-wanted toy and he already knew there was no way anyone was going to prise it away from her.

'So what have you brought for Luke?' Bobbie asked her twin absently an hour later as they all sat down together for their meal.

Grinning at her brother-in-law, Samantha told him, 'It's a golf club, a new one, I don't believe you can get it over here yet.'

'Not an "iron overlord,"' Luke breathed hopefully.

'The very same,' Samantha confirmed, laughing as he got up and came round the table to hug her and then demand, 'Where is it? I...'

'Not until after you have finished your meal, Luke,' Bobbie mock frowned at him.

By nine o'clock Samantha was ready to concede that her long flight had caught up with her.

'If you're really sure you don't mind if I go to bed...?'

'Of course we don't mind,' Bobbie reassured her.

'What's wrong?' Luke asked Bobbie an hour later as he handed her the mug of chocolate he had just made her.

'I don't know...it's just...Sam's up to something...'

'Like what?'

'I don't know and there's no point in my asking, she'd just clam up on me, but *something's* going on...'

'Twin telepathy?' Luke teased.

'Something's bothering her, Luke, she's put her guard up to prevent me finding out about it but I *know* it's

there... I wish she could find her special someone... She
so desperately wants children...'

'Mmm...now that I did notice.'

'Well, at least I've got lots of things planned to enter-
tain her whilst she's here...'

'Mmm...I'm afraid there's a slight problem on that
score,' Luke told his wife quietly.

Bobbie looked questioningly at him.

'Luke...' she began.

'Yes, I know we agreed that I would take time off to
look after Francesca so that you would be free to spend
time with Sam, but...'

'But *what*...'

'The Dillinger case comes up for trial next week and
I'm going to be in court.'

'Oh, Luke, no...' Bobbie wailed.

'Bobbie, I'm sorry, but you know the way things are.'

She did, of course she did, Luke was a barrister and if
one of his cases came to court then he had to be there.

'Sam's here for several weeks and with any luck the
case should be over in two,' Luke comforted her.

'Well, I just hope that *Sam* understands,' Bobbie told
him.

CHAPTER FIVE

'I REALLY am sorry, Sam,' Bobbie apologised to her sister, 'but there's nothing that Luke can do.'

They had just finished eating breakfast and Bobbie had explained to her twin that she wasn't going to be as free to devote her time to her as she had hoped.

To her relief Samantha seemed completely unfazed by her news.

'Don't worry about it,' she told her sunnily. 'Besides,' she added, her voice and eyes softening, 'you and the coming baby mean far more to me than socialising and treats. As a matter of fact, James has actually offered his services as an escort should I need one.'

With a shaky smile Bobbie reached out to cover her twin's hand with her own. 'I *am* feeling more tired with this baby, and both my doctor and Luke have insisted that I ought to rest,' she admitted, her face brightening as she added, 'But at least you'll have James to take you about.'

James and Samantha had always got on well together.

'Well, hopefully Luke's case should be over in a fortnight and...'

'Mmm...well that should be long enough.'

Samantha bit her lip as she realised she had spoken her thoughts out loud.

'For what?' Bobbie asked her curiously. 'I...'

'Oh, nothing... I just meant that a fortnight should be long enough for the case to be concluded,' Samantha fibbed airily, quickly redirecting Bobbie's attention by asking her, 'How's Fran doing at school now? You were concerned that she wasn't being stretched enough.'

'Mmm… I was, but Luke says that she is only four and he doesn't want her being pushed too hard and that he'd rather she exercised her own curiosity naturally.'

'Well, he does have a point. Look at the way the pair of us ran wild whenever we went to Gramps, and it certainly didn't do us any harm.'

'No, I suppose not.'

'Olivia's invited us over for lunch today.'

'Has she? How are she and Caspar?' Samantha asked affectionately and within several minutes the sisters were deeply immersed in a detailed update of what was happening within the Haslewich and Chester branches of the Crighton family.

'It's a pity that Grandma Ruth can't be here right now,' Bobbie commented.

'Mmm… I was looking forward to seeing her and Gramps,' Samantha admitted. 'But I can understand why she felt she had to go to Pembrokeshire. How is Ann?'

Ann Crighton, Hugh Crighton's wife, had been involved in an accident which had resulted in her being hospitalised for several weeks.

'Well, she's at home now and the doctors have confirmed that she will make a full recovery, but Hugh's terrified that she's going to try to do too much. She's been forbidden to climb any stairs or to do anything more than walk very slowly and gently until the damage to her back heals properly.'

'It's frightening to realise just how much damage even the slightest car accident can cause.' Samantha gave a small shiver. 'According to what Gran has told Mom, it was just a simple shunt and the car which hit Ann's was hardly moving at all.'

'Yes, I know,' Bobbie agreed soberly. 'It certainly made me feel very wary about taking Francesca out anywhere in the car for weeks afterwards and I can understand, too, why Hugh asked Grandma Ruth for her help in keeping Ann occupied whilst she's recovering.'

'They're such a lovely couple and although Gran never says so, I suspect that she secretly prefers Hugh to Ben, even though Ben's her full blood brother and Hugh only a half.'

'Mmm...but then just because there's a full blood relationship between siblings, it doesn't necessarily mean that they are going to like one another.'

This was said so gravely that Samantha gave her twin a quick look before teasing, 'And what conclusions am I supposed to draw from that, sister dear?'

Bobbie looked at her, her face relaxing into a smile.

'Don't worry, I'm not trying to say I don't like *you*...hate you sometimes, maybe...' she teased back and then, shaking her head, she confided, 'No...it's not us...but...'

'But what?' Samantha encouraged when she fell silent.

'Well, you know how it can be with families sometimes...brothers and sisters, siblings...just don't always get on...'

'Sibling rivalry... Well, we've certainly had our fair share of that in the Crighton family. I mean, if you want a classic example just look at Jon and Jenny's family. Louise and Katie positively loathed Max at one time, and...'

'Yes, yes, I know what you're saying but it isn't...' Bobbie stopped again and then started to trace an abstract pattern on the wooden kitchen table with her fingertip.

'It's Fran and the new baby,' she admitted huskily after

several seconds. 'I think she's starting to get a little bit jealous—even before he or she is born.'

She looked so upset.

'But surely, Bobbie, that's only natural,' Samantha defended her niece immediately. 'She's bound to feel a little bit jealous,' Samantha told her twin robustly. 'Everything will be all right, though.'

'Yes, I know you're right,' she agreed, adding gently, 'You will make such a wonderful mother, Sam.'

Although Samantha laughed, a little later on whilst her twin was on the telephone to Olivia confirming the arrangements for their visit, she couldn't help feeling a small stab of envy. Here was her sister, her twin, talking about having her second baby whilst she didn't even have the means of having her first yet. But, with a bit of luck, she soon would have, she comforted herself.

Everything she had heard and seen of James during the drive back from the airport yesterday had confirmed the decision she had already made. There was no doubt about it. He was *perfect* father material. Add to that the fact that she genuinely liked him and enjoyed his company, the way she could so easily see the two of them meshing together and becoming a very happy and contented couple, and suddenly Samantha was very impatient to see him again and to put her plan fully into motion. Okay, so she hadn't fallen *in* love with him but love, after all, came in very many disguises.

There was nothing *morally* wrong in what she was planning and if she had not been able to see in James' eyes how very easily he could be encouraged to fall in love with her she would not in any way have contemplated going ahead with her plans.

She had made up her mind—it was time to put to one side her dreams of meeting her perfect other half. She

might not be headily in love with James in the same way
that her twin had been, still was, with his brother Luke,
but she liked him and enjoyed his company, he was just
so relaxing and pleasant to be with she just couldn't imagine anyone *not* finding him so, other than Rosemary.
Heavens, but she had never seen anyone cause such an
intense and explosive reaction in him. He really did dislike the girl. Poor Rosemary.

'We'd better make a move,' Bobbie warned Samantha
when she had finished her telephone call.

'It's gone ten now and we'll have to be back by two
so that I can pick Francesca up on time.'

'Will Olivia and Caspar have any more children, do
you think?' Samantha asked Bobbie conversationally half
an hour later as Bobbie drove towards Haslewich.

'I don't know. She works full-time now as you know
and she and Uncle Jon keep on talking about taking on a
new partner, but although neither of them will admit it,
the main thing that's holding them both back from doing
so is the fact that since its inception the partnership has
always only been family members. There's a good crop
of young Crightons growing up now who might one day
want to qualify as solicitors and join the business, but
right now…Tullah, Saul's wife works part-time with them
two days.'

'Can't they take someone on as an assistant rather than
a full partner?' Samantha queried.

'Well, they could and that's exactly what Max has been
urging his father to do. It's looking increasingly as though
Jack will opt to train as a solicitor and join the business
but that's still several years away and at the moment they
are so busy that Jenny's complaining that she hardly ever
sees Jon.'

'What about Joss, has he any plans for his future?' Samantha asked her twin.

Joss, Jon and Jenny's younger son, was hotly tipped in the family to become their leading light in the legal world and Samantha knew that Bobbie had a very soft spot for the teenager who had been the first member of the Crighton family she had met on her first visit to Haslewich.

'At least a dozen,' Bobbie grinned. 'He's gorgeous, Sam…such a very special person, so special in fact that it's hard sometimes to remember not to overlook Jack.'

'Mmm… I wonder what happened to Jack's father David. Does Jack ever talk about him?'

David Crighton, Jon's twin brother, was Jack and Olivia's father and whilst recuperating from a heart attack he had simply walked out of the lives of his family and made little attempt to get in touch with them since.

Olivia, Samantha knew, had no real wish for her father to make a reappearance in their lives. Before his disappearance she and Jon had discovered that he had been fraudulently helping himself to money from one of their client's accounts. It was only thanks to Ruth's intervention that the whole unpleasant matter had been resolved without a scandal and Samantha knew from Olivia's own comments that she had never really forgiven her father for what he had done.

Her mother, who had divorced David in his absence, was now remarried and living in the south of England. Olivia had never been close to either of her parents and Jack had, of his own free will, chosen to live with his aunt and uncle rather than with his mother.

'So, you don't think that Olivia will have any more children, then,' Samantha repeated.

'I think she'd like to and I know that Caspar would—

his work allows him to have more time to spend with them than Livvy's does but, to be honest, I suspect it's rather a sensitive issue between them at the moment. They were due to go on holiday this year to visit Caspar's family in the States, but it had to be cancelled because Livvy is just so busy.

'Haslewich has become rather a mini boom town. The extended motorway system has meant that several international industries have moved into the area and, of course, that means extra jobs, which means increased property development. Property prices have risen and on the outskirts of the town they're currently just about to open one of these specialised shopping villages, all designer outlets and very, very smart.

'Not that that was without problems—you ask James. He's just won a very involved case for one of his clients against one of the contractors on the development.'

'I can't imagine James prosecuting. He always seems so gentle and compassionate. Although…'

'Although what?' Bobbie questioned interestedly as she slowed down for the motorway exit to Haslewich.

'Well, we called on his parents on the way back from the airport and there was a girl there—Rosemary. I've never seen James react so antagonistically to anyone…mind you, her attitude towards *him* was extremely…'

'…provocative?' Bobbie suggested.

Samantha looked at her. 'Aggressive, *I* was about to say… Do you know her, Bobbie?'

'I've met her. She was visiting Luke and James' parents last Christmas and I had gone to see them with Francesca. Francesca wasn't very well and Rosemary was absolutely sweet with her. She's just recently qualified as a doctor, you know, and Pat was telling me that she is hoping to specialise in the area of paediatrics within the surgery complex. She certainly has a wonderful way with children.'

'You liked her, then,' Samantha stated.

'Well…yes, I did, but I know what you mean about her and James, they certainly strike sparks off one another. Apparently she spent several months living with Henry and Pat whilst she was a teenager. Her parents were working abroad at the time, Luke wasn't living at home then, but James was, and the two of them just didn't hit it off together.'

'Mmm… Oh, isn't this the most beautiful scenery,' Samantha enthused as she glanced out of the car window to look appreciatively at the gently rolling Cheshire countryside.

'Very,' Bobbie agreed.

'It's so peaceful,' Samantha stressed.

Bobbie laughed. 'It might be now, wait until you get to Livvy's!'

Olivia and Caspar's home was outside the town of Haslewich, a pretty, long low collection of buildings surrounded by a large garden and fields.

As Bobbie brought the car to a halt on the driveway, Olivia was opening the front door and coming hurrying to meet them.

Slim and energetic, her bobbed hair gleamed in the sunshine and a swift smile curled her mouth as she welcomed them.

'Bobbie… Sam…' She hugged each of them in turn and then gestured towards the house.

'I thought we'd have lunch in the garden, it's such a lovely day. I nearly had to cancel,' Olivia confessed as she led the way through the house to the doors which opened out onto the pretty brick patio.

'I was due in court with one of my clients last week and the case was put back originally until today, but the case currently being heard is still ongoing—fortunately.'

'Do you do much court work?' Samantha asked Olivia as they settled themselves in comfortable chairs and Olivia poured them all some coffee.

'An awful lot. I didn't used to but increasingly these days, yes. I'm afraid that it's becoming rather a bone of contention between me and Caspar, primarily because it means I can't always structure my working life to fit in with his.'

'Mmm...and I guess you daren't hire another live-in nanny just in case she runs off with another of your sexy cousins,' Bobbie said teasingly.

All three of them laughed, remembering that Bobbie had worked for a time for Olivia and Caspar when she had first arrived in Haslewich.

'Mmm...well there is always that, but although I've had help from time to time, Caspar and I both feel that we want to bring the children up ourselves. The trouble is that, right now, Caspar is doing rather more of the parenting than I am and that leads to problems between us. I get jealous,' she admitted ruefully. 'I know it sounds silly and it's certainly very unmodern of me, but I could cry when the children run to Caspar with their scraped knees and their tears instead of to me.'

'Couldn't you lessen the number of hours you work?' Samantha suggested practically.

Olivia rolled her eyes expressively. 'I wish... As it is I'm conscious of how often Jon takes home my workload to allow me to have extra time off. No, we both know that the only real answer is to take on at least one and maybe two qualified solicitors, but the problem is that anyone we take on of the calibre we need would automatically want to become a partner somewhere down the line and, whilst Ben's alive, well even if he wasn't, I guess that both Jon and I are Crighton enough not to want to dilute the partnership.

'Of course we could turn down work but...' She pulled a face. '*That* goes so much against the grain. No, at the moment we're in a strictly no win situation and no matter how many junior assistants we might take on, when it comes down to it, Jon and I are the only senior members of staff. However, today I am having a day off...

'How are your family?' she asked Samantha, changing the subject.

'They're fine. Mom and Dad are looking forward to Dad's retirement later in the year and to their vacation over here, of course.'

'Mmm... We're all looking forward to seeing them, especially Aunt Ruth of course. How is the divine Liam, by the way.'

Sam's eyebrows rose at this description of her currently least favourite person. Not even to Bobbie had she confided her reaction to that unprecedented and totally unexpected kiss Liam had given her before she had left home.

'He's fine. He'll shortly be running for State Governor.'

'Governor. He'll be the sexiest one the union has ever had.' Olivia rolled her eyes again. She had, of course, met Liam at Bobbie and Luke's wedding—renewing their acquaintanceship when she and Caspar had visited the States some years ago.

'Sexy! Liam!' Sam started to expostulate and then stopped quickly veiling her eyes to conceal her expression. *She* didn't think Liam was sexy, of course she didn't, but the memory of that unprovoked kiss was still lingering disturbingly not just in her mind but on her senses as well.

*   *   *

The telephone was ringing when they walked into the house on their return from their visit to Olivia. Bobbie picked up the receiver and then pulled a face, holding it out to Samantha.

'It's for you,' she told her dryly, eyebrows raised. 'It's James.'

'James,' Samantha exclaimed in a pleased voice as she took the receiver from her twin and deliberately turned her back towards her.

'Tonight…yes…I'd love to…' she agreed. 'What time? Yes, I guess eight will be fine.

'James is taking me out for dinner tonight,' she told her twin after she had concluded her call. 'He says there's a new restaurant opened on the river which is very highly acclaimed.'

Bobbie opened her mouth as though she was about to say something and then closed it again as she surveyed her sister's flushed face and happy eyes.

James and Samantha?

Well, her twin would certainly never find a more easy-going nor indulgent partner than James, and Sam would certainly benefit from someone in her life who would ground her a little, but was James strong enough to match Samantha? Samantha could sometimes get a little carried away with her ideas and plans and didn't always think them through properly from a practical point of view, as Bobbie well knew. She was inclined to be impulsive and idealistic and she was also extremely strong-willed. She needed a man who would not just understand and love her but who would share and match the deeply passionate and intense side of her nature, as well. A pretty tall order, Bobbie knew, but to her mind Sam deserved the best.

James was a darling and nothing would make Bobbie happier than to see him settled and married. He had already suffered disappointments in love and if anyone deserved to be loved, then it was certainly James. But was Samantha the right one for him? James liked order and calm; he liked routine and neatness, as a Virgo he tended to be almost even a little bit overfussy on occasions. His desk, his office, and his home were models of orderliness and pristine neatness.

Sam, on the other hand, could cheerfully live in the kind of chaos that made other people either stare in envy or grit their teeth in despair, depending on their own natures.

She was headstrong, vital, vibrant, swinging from one extreme to another in the space of a handful of minutes. She possessed a joie de vivre that other people either adored or loathed, there were no half measures with Samantha, whereas James epitomised the spirit of compromise. Still, they did say that opposites attract.

'If you're going near the river I'd take a warm jacket with you,' Bobbie warned her. 'It can be quite cool near the water in the evening.'

Predictably Samantha was still upstairs getting ready when James arrived to collect her.

Bobbie let him in and hugged and kissed him lovingly.

'Sam won't be long,' she assured him.

James gave her a small smile.

'Good, I've booked the table for eight-thirty which just leaves us time to drive there and order a drink at the bar before we eat.'

Rather ruefully Bobbie looked away, relieved to hear her twin's feet on the stairs as Samantha came hurrying down.

She had certainly dressed for the occasion, Bobbie reflected as she studied her sister.

The pretty linen wrap skirt emphasised the female shape of Sam's body and the toning effect of cream on cream with the softly draped top she was wearing created an image of soft delicacy whilst Sam's freshly washed tousled curls gave her an appealing youthful air.

'Where's your jacket?' Bobbie asked her as Sam passed her in the hall.

'If I get cold I'll have to borrow James',' Samantha told her sotto voce, smiling mischievously as she saw her twin's expression.

'You'll need a jacket,' James warned her, unconsciously echoing Bobbie's comment to her earlier.

Samantha hesitated, torn between protesting that she wasn't a child and that if she chose not to wear a jacket then it was *her* choice and allowing herself to bask in the unfamiliarity of James' male concern.

In the end the latter won out and she hurried back upstairs, returning with a soft cashmere wraparound knitted jacket draped around her shoulders.

'Very nice,' Bobbie approved.

'You look lovely,' James told her quietly and sincerely, smiling tenderly at her as he reached out and gently straightened the ruffled edge of her knit so that both sides were equally matched.

Samantha's eyebrows rose but she didn't make any comment.

'We'd better go,' James was informing her. 'We don't want to be late for our table.'

Bobbie, who knew that her twin had raised being late to an art form, forbore to make any comment, but instead mentally crossed her fingers as she wished the pair of them a pleasant evening.

'*Sam* and *James?*' Luke exclaimed later when Bobbie was telling him what had happened. His eyebrows rose and he gave her a droll look. 'You *have* to be joking. James knows to the last pair exactly how many socks he has and where they are. I would be astonished if your sister could find a single item in her wardrobe in less than a week!'

'Mmm...you could have a point,' Bobbie allowed. 'Except that Sam would be more likely to have most of her clothes lying in a heap on her bedroom chair or floor,' Bobbie admitted with a grin.

'I rest my case,' Luke told her mock solemnly.

'Yes, but opposites do attract,' Bobbie reminded him hopefully.

'Mmm...they also have some of the most spectacularly messy and acrimonious divorce cases that ever come to court. Take it from me, I've seen them.'

'Mmm...well, James seems pretty keen...'

'Maybe *now* he does, wait until Sam has dropped ice cream on his suit, lost her purse and locked him out of his own car,' Luke suggested.

Since her twin had on the occasion of her last visit committed all three of those crimes against Luke, Bobbie felt unable to say very much in defence of her sister.

'James would drive Sam mad,' Luke told her more seriously. 'She'd end up resenting or even loathing him.'

'But if they fell in love,' Bobbie protested.

'With the idea of being in love, yes, but with each other—no!'

In the soft shadows of the restaurant's private walled garden Samantha started to put her plan into action. The romantic venue James had chosen for their meal was certainly a good start and she was enjoying having James fuss round her, checking that she was warm enough, that her chair was comfortable, that the menu was to her liking. It felt wonderful to be so thoroughly pampered.

'James, you're spoiling me,' she told him softly as she leaned across the table to cover his hand with her own just fleetingly enough to be subtly intimate without lingering too long or being too obvious.

It would be quite in order for her to kiss James goodnight as a thank you for her evening out she decided judiciously as the waiter took their order—and *when* she did...!

A naughty little smile curled her mouth.

'You know, you frighten me a little when you look like that,' James told her ruefully.

'Me—frighten you!' Sam rolled her eyes wickedly.

CHAPTER SIX

'So, IN your opinion, Toni, your professional opinion that is...' Liam stressed, 'I'm not going to win the governorship unless I have a wife.'

They were seated opposite one another in the privacy of Liam's apartment since Toni Davis had insisted that the subject she wanted to discuss with him was far too vital to the success of his campaign for them to risk anyone else overhearing it.

He watched as she arched an eyebrow and gave him the benefit of her perfect profile whilst making a slightly depreciative moue.

'I couldn't say *that,* but there is no doubt that amongst a certain section of the voters a Governor who has the right kind of wife is considered to be preferable to one who doesn't.'

'The *right* kind of wife?' Liam asked her, his own eyebrows lifting. Toni gave him a small intimate look.

'Liam, I've worked in PR a good while *and* in Washington, we both know that to be successful, a politician needs to have the right kind of partnership support. I'm sure we've *both* seen very able politicians failing to make the grade because of...problems in their domestic lives...

'Your voters feel that a married Governor will be more in tune with their own lives and needs. You and I both know that it takes a very special kind of woman to fully understand the stresses and pressures that go with high office.

'In my view,' Toni Davis continued, 'the very best kind of successful political marriages are those where both partners are working together for a common goal and where both partners understand their roles and one another. For a man in high office it is vitally important that his wife is totally committed to his success and to him.'

'Isn't that a rather old-fashioned point of view?' Liam checked her.

'Old-fashioned it may be, but it works,' Toni told him firmly.

'So you believe that a politician should marry for expediency rather than for love?' Liam challenged her.

'Romantic love seldom lasts and can cause far too many problems. A successful politician doesn't have time to waste on emotion,' Toni told him calmly. 'You're a very sensible man, Liam, and an ambitious man, I know, so I'm sure you understand what I'm saying.'

Liam gave her a thoughtful look.

Oh, he understood what she was saying right enough. From the moment he had picked her up from the airport Toni had made it clear that it wasn't just her professional expertise in public relations she was prepared to put at Liam's disposal. She might not have come right out and said that she would like to be the Governor's wife, but she had certainly made it plenty clear in a number of other ways.

Stephen Miller had told Liam privately that he had heard from a source in Washington that Toni had, for several years, been having an affair with a very high-ranking Congressman.

'He was a lot older than her and his wife was terminally ill. Word is that she was prepared to sit it out and wait to become his second wife but that when, instead of asking her to marry him, he upped and married someone else she vowed that she would find a way of getting even with him.'

'And did she...'

'Well, he isn't a Congressman anymore...'

'Mmm...nice lady!'

'She certainly knows what she wants,' Stephen Miller had agreed.

As Liam watched her gravely whilst she warmed to her theme and started to list the many advantages to the kind of marriage she was proposing, he reflected that there was, in all honesty, something to be said for what she was suggesting and that she would most definitely make an admirable wife for an ambitious politician.

Unfortunately, there were two very good reasons why *he* didn't feel able to take her up on her proposals.

'Well, I take your point,' he interrupted her firmly, 'but I guess I'm the old-fashioned kind myself and I kinda think that I'd be cheating the voters just a little if I married purely to get their vote. I guess you *could* say it was a matter of pride. You see, I'd want to be loved for my *self* both by the voters *and* by my wife,' he told her gently.

She was still staring at him with her face unfalteringly flushed and her mouth open several seconds later as he strolled towards the door and held it open for her.

A little later in the day he had occasion to call at the Governor's house to see Stephen Miller.

'He's in his study,' Sarah Jane told Liam with a smile, asking him fondly, 'How did your meeting go with Toni this morning? Stephen says that she's absolutely determined that you'll win the governorship.'

'Well, right now I guess she isn't feeling too pleased with me,' Liam admitted.

When Sarah Jane waited, he elucidated, 'I can't marry just to secure the governorship. Toni's insistence that the

right kind of wife will secure it for me may be correct,
but...'

As he spoke his glance lingered briefly on a photograph
of Samantha on one of the tables in the hallway.

Following his gaze Sarah Jane smiled ruefully. In it
Samantha was wearing her graduation gown and for once
she looked almost a little awed and unfamiliarly subdued
by the gravitas of the moment.

'You know, Liam, there have been times when I worried that I might be hindering Stephen's career. It's no
secret to you that I'm looking forward to him retiring.'

'What is obvious to *me* is that Stephen's love for you
and his family means far, far more to him than being a
politician,' Liam told her truthfully.

'Sam used to be passionately resentful of the way her
father's career took him away from us all when she was
younger,' Sarah Jane commented ruefully as she walked
across to her daughter's photograph and picked it up.

'Yup, I remember, and it wasn't just his *career* she
resented so passionately,' Liam replied dryly.

Sarah Jane laughed. 'Oh dear, yes, she did go through
a phase of blaming you for his absences. She was jealous
of you, of course, because you got to spend time in
Washington with him whilst she couldn't.

'Poor Sam,' Sarah Jane sighed. 'She'd certainly never
make a politician's wife. I used to think that once she
grew up she'd be less impulsive and...intense...but... I'll
go and get Stephen for you, Liam,' she offered, putting
the photograph back and walking towards his office.

In her absence Liam picked up the picture of Sam.

Sarah Jane was right, Sam would never make a politician's wife. She would never toe the line, never keep a
tactful silence when an issue was raised about which she
felt passionately, and she felt passionately about every

issue there was. She would never put her husband's career before her own dearly held beliefs, she would never tell her children, *their* children, not to bother their father with their problems because he was a very busy and important man. She would never allow her man, her mate, to get the idea that she could be kept discreetly in the background and she would certainly never, ever, accept the kind of cold clinical and entirely rational relationship which Toni had recently outlined to him.

Oh yes, there were a hundred, no, a thousand reasons why Sam would not make a good politician's wife.

He was carefully replacing the photograph in its original position when Stephen came hurrying towards him, Sarah Jane not far behind.

'Toni's just been on the phone to me,' he began, but Liam stopped him.

'Yes, and I can guess what she had to say but what *I* told her stands. The voters of this country have to want me as their Governor as I am,' he told Stephen firmly. 'But that isn't what I've come to tell you—I'm taking a couple of weeks leave.'

Stephen stared at him.

'What! Right *now,* in the middle of the campaign…'

'The campaign can run quite happily without me for a while. In fact, you never know, the voters might discover that an undiluted diet of Lee Calder might give them a craving for a different kind of politician.'

'Mmm… Well, you could be right and you certainly won't get any time to take any leave if you do get the governorship. Where are you planning to go?'

'Ireland,' Liam told him promptly.

'Ireland…' Both the Millers stared at him.

'I've been meaning to visit over there for a

while…trace my roots, that kind of thing,' Liam told them vaguely.

'Ireland, but it's only just across the Irish sea from Cheshire,' Sarah Jane told him enthusiastically. 'You could perhaps fit in a visit to Bobbie whilst you're there. I know she'd *love* to see you.'

Liam gave a small shrug.

'Bobbie might, but I doubt that Sam would…'

'Well that could be so.' Sarah Jane paused and then laughed. 'Although from what I hear from Bobbie, Sam *is* rather preoccupied at the moment. She's been seeing rather a lot of James since she arrived.'

As Samantha's parents exchanged smiles, neither of them saw the way Liam's mouth tightened nor the look he flashed the silent photograph of their daughter.

Seated in her sister's kitchen Samantha leaned her chin into her hand and gave a small disconsolate sigh. So far her plans were not going entirely the way she wanted.

Oh, James was proving to be everything she had anticipated that he would be, a thoughtful and protective escort when he took her out and an entertaining and interesting companion, but no matter how hard she tried she just couldn't seem to advance their relationship to a more intimate level.

Take the first night he had asked her out, for instance. After they had left the restaurant they had strolled alongside the river, the perfect romantic setting. Samantha had leant a little against James, smiling warmly and encouragingly at him when he had stopped walking and turned to face her, but instead of taking her in his arms and kissing her as she had expected, he had started to frown a little and caution her that her knit was in danger of slipping off her shoulders.

She had been so irritated by his overcautious behaviour that later on, when he *had* moved to take her in his arms when he had stopped his car outside Luke and Bobbie's home, she had pretended not to be aware of his intentions, slipping out of the car before he could stop her and then kissing him coolly and distantly on the cheek before bidding him a stiff goodnight outside the front door.

Later on she had regretted giving in to her chagrin and irritation but, of course, by then it had been too late.

The following day, at her insistence, he had taken her to the zoo, but the antics of the animals had quite plainly not been to his taste and he had cut their visit short, suggesting instead that she might like to visit Haslewich's salt museum which he was sure she would find far more worthwhile.

As Samantha was coming to discover, underneath James' apparent easygoing gentleness there was a markedly determined, not to say stubborn, streak. It wasn't that he was either domineering or dictatorial, it was simply that he could at times adopt a smiling loftiness which irritated her into the kind of rebellious behaviour she thought she had left behind with her teens. And yet he was everything she *knew* she ought to want. She only had to see him with Olivia's children and Bobbie's Francesca, to see what a wonderful father he would make.

An added complication to her plans was Rosemary. Despite her avowed dislike of him and her engagement, she tried to attach herself to them with all the persistence and much the same effect as an unwanted burr.

'Poor Rosemary, I'm afraid she finds it rather dull being with someone so much older than herself,' James' mother had commented indulgently to Samantha the previous day when, for the third time Rosemary had insisted on accompanying them.

If Rosemary was so bored then why didn't she go home to her own life and her own friends? Samantha longed to ask, but she managed to keep her views to herself.

'She and James can't bear one another so why she insists on attaching herself to us I just don't know,' she had told Bobbie furiously the previous evening when, at the last minute, Rosemary had prevailed upon James' mother to ask if she could be included in their outing to an open-air play—one of a series which were held every summer at a pretty local Elizabethan manor house.

Bobbie had given her a telling look.

But at the weekend James was taking her to the Grosvenor for dinner and *that* was an invitation she intended to make sure Rosemary did *not* gate crash.

James lived in the city within walking distance of the Grosvenor, Chester's most prestigious hotel, and Samantha had privately decided to boldly suggest after they had had dinner that James might show her over his home. If *that* didn't give him a hint of what she had in mind then nothing would!

It was not that she was planning to deliberately seduce him. Of course not. And anyway, she had seen from the expression in his eyes when he looked at her that he found her attractive and he had certainly hinted at as much with the compliments he had paid her. No, it was just that she felt their relationship needed a small nudge in the right direction to move it on a little faster than it was presently progressing.

James just wasn't the type to force the pace. He was far too gentlemanly for that, and so *she* needed to make it clear to him that... That what? That she wanted him to take her to bed?

Samantha started to frown. *Did* she? *Did* she want them to become lovers?

Well, of course she did, otherwise how on earth was she going to conceive their child. Ultimately they would *have* to... *Have to?*

'You're looking very pensive.'

Samantha looked at her sister.

'No, not really... I was just wondering what to wear when James takes me to dinner at the Grosvenor on Saturday.'

'Mmm... Well, it should be something smart. The Grosvenor's clientele *is* very elegant.'

'Mmm...' Samantha didn't want to admit to her twin that it was more what she should wear to get the right impression over to *James* than to impress the other diners, that was concerning her.

'Mom rang whilst you were out earlier. You'll never guess what...'

'So tell me,' Samantha invited.

'Liam's in Ireland.'

'Liam's *where?*'

'In Ireland taking a vacation and looking up his roots.'

'But Liam never takes a vacation. *Never.* And what about the campaign?'

Bobbie shrugged.

'*I* only know what Mom told me. Oh, she did say though, that that PR woman has gone back to Washington.'

'Oh... Maybe Liam's gone to Ireland to look for a wife,' Samantha suggested cynically.

'Oh, Sam, you aren't being very fair to Liam.'

'He *wants* to be Governor, you can't deny that.'

'No, but he wants the governorship as much for Dad as for himself.'

Bobbie saw her sister's disbelieving expression and insisted, 'It's true. Liam knows how much Dad wants to have him take over from him, how much it would mean to him to be able to retire knowing that he's leaving the state in safe hands, *and* he knows, too, how much Mom has been looking forward to Dad retiring.'

'Liam is Dad's assistant, you're making it sound more as though he's a member of the family.'

'Well, *isn't* he? You *know* how much Mom and Dad both think of him.'

'Too much if you ask me,' Samantha muttered half under her breath. 'I can certainly remember how often they took his side against me.'

'When? Oh, you mean like that time you wanted to go out with the high school jock and Liam told the folks that he'd got a pretty bad reputation. Liam was just trying to protect you, that was all.'

'To *protect* me...' Samantha rolled her eyes. 'Oh, yeah...'

'You're too hard on him, Sam. I know how much Dad values him and Dad is a very good judge of character. Grandma Ruth and Gramps both think a lot of him, as well.'

'So... That's because he's made sure they've only seen the *good* side of him,' Samantha told her.

'Oh, Sam...' Bobbie laughed and shook her head. 'And when I think of the *crush* you used to have on him.'

Bobbie gave her twin a startled look.

'You *aren't* still holding a grudge against him because he didn't return your feelings, are you? You *must* know how impossible it would have been for him to respond to you, not just morally but just about every which way there is. You were under age, you were his employer's daughter, you were...'

'I was damn near six feet tall and looked more like a boy than a girl and I wore braces. Yes, I know, but he need not have treated me as though…as though…as though I was some kind of joke,' Samantha seethed.

'As though you were some kind of joke. No, he never did that.'

'He did, too,' Samantha told her. 'He laughed at me and he…'

'Samantha, he was just trying to diffuse the situation, to let you down gently. I guess…'

'Anyway, for your information I am *not* holding a grudge against him. As a matter of fact—well, I guess you're right and he *is* the right person to take over from Dad and I hope he finds himself a wife in Ireland,' she added generously.

'You do. Well, you can tell him so yourself when he comes over to visit with us at the weekend.'

'He's doing *what*,' Samantha demanded, staring at her.

'He's coming over to visit with us,' Bobbie repeated calmly. 'Apparently Mom suggested it.'

'Liam here! Liam's coming here, to Haslewich!' Samantha started to worry her bottom lip. She still had disturbing flashbacks to those moments she had spent in his arms when he had kissed her and, illogically and *very* dangerously, they always seemed to surface when she was with James! She forced herself to give a small nonchalant shrug.

'Well, it's a pity but I shall probably miss him. Have you forgotten I'm going to the Grosvenor with James on Saturday.' *Going* to the Grosvenor and *planning* to stay over with James although no one other than her knew about *that* plan as yet.

'No, you won't. He's actually going to be staying at the Grosvenor.'

Samantha felt her heart start to sink. She and Liam might have buried their old differences but…but she had confided in him in a moment of weakness, exposed to him her fears and vulnerabilities and she had no wish now to have him watching superciliously and knowingly whilst she put into action her plans for her future with James.

'In fact, I'm thinking about arranging to have a family lunch party at the Grosvenor on Sunday.'

'If Liam finds a wife whilst he's in Ireland and he brings her over, we could make it an engagement party,' Samantha suggested sarcastically. 'Maybe you ought to order a cake.'

'Uh-huh. And would that be for Liam and his intended or for you and James?' Bobbie demanded teasingly, adding with a sideways look, 'Have you told him about your yen to make love out in the open yet, because...'

'That was just a childish fantasy,' Samantha told her loftily, but her face had gone pink nonetheless. It was true that she had always had a private fantasy of making love out in the open beneath the sky, somewhere private and secret, a sacred almost a special place which would belong to her and her lover alone.

A fantasy was just what it was though. Somehow she could not see James sharing it with her. Fantasies didn't always translate very well into real life.

A little uncertainly Samantha surveyed her reflection in the long pier mirror in Bobbie's guest bedroom.

The seductively feminine underwear she had bought in Boston had seemed like a good idea at the time but now that she was wearing it...surely the silky satin was far finer and provocative than she had remembered it. She frowned as she saw the way it clung to her curves, lovingly outlining every detail of her body.

'Sam... I've just remembered... Wow!' Bobbie came

to a full stop as she hurried unceremoniously into her twin's bedroom, her eyes widening as she looked at her.

'The dress I'm wearing is silk jersey and it needs something special underneath it,' Samantha began defensively, but she could see from Bobbie's raised eyebrows and wide grin that she was not convincing her.

'Ever heard of a plain simple serviceable body?' Bobbie asked her dryly.

'They didn't have one in my size. You know how difficult it is getting one long enough,' Samantha defended herself.

'Have I said a word?' Bobbie asked virtuously. 'If you choose to wear sexy underwear then far be it from me… You always did have a penchant for…' She stopped and giggled.

'Remember that fuss you made when you had your crush on Liam when Mom took you to buy a new training bra. You refused to have it and begged her to let you have a push-up padded style instead.'

'That was years ago,' Samantha objected, 'and besides, Mom refused…'

'Well, you certainly don't need any help in improving your curves now,' Bobbie told her forthrightly. 'So where is it then?' she demanded.

'Where's what?' Samantha asked her puzzled.

'The dress…the dress that demands the wearing of such sexy underwear,' Bobbie told her, tongue-in-cheek.

'It's here.' Turning round Samantha walked over to the wardrobe and removed the dress she was planning to wear that evening. Completely plain in heavy vanilla silk jersey, its slashed cowl-necked style made Bobbie's eyes widen in envy.

'Hey if you ever get tired of it, you can junk it in my direction puleeze…'

Samantha laughed.

'Let me see it on,' Bobbie commanded.

Dutifully Samantha took it off the hanger and slipped it over her head.

The soft vanilla fabric settled down over her body as though it had been made expressly for her, the heavy fabric draping perfectly over her curves.

She had chosen the bra, carefully picking one with a low back, knowing that the deep vee of the dress would expose a normal bra.

'It's wonderful,' Bobbie breathed, and then frowned. 'Can you step out of it?' she asked Samantha.

Her sister stared at her.

'I don't know, I haven't tried. Why do you ask.'

Bobbie grinned.

'Well, it's just that there's something seriously sexy about a dress that can be slithered out of. You know the kind that just somehow falls to the floor of its own accord. Although,' she paused and eyed her twin judiciously, 'I suppose there is *something* to be said for one that needs an extra pair of hands to aid its removal.'

'I did *not* buy this dress with…with anything like that in mind,' Samantha told her firmly.

'Anything like "that"… You mean, sex?' Bobbie teased, round-eyed.

'It's six o'clock, James is picking me up at half past,' Samantha warned her, 'and he'll expect me to be ready on time.'

'Okay, okay, I get the message. Subject closed, although…' As she headed for the door she paused and told her thoughtfully, 'if you want my opinion that bit of frivolous sexy nonsense you're wearing is very much more Liam than James!'

'For the last time, I did not choose my underwear with a man in mind…any man…'

'Who says I was talking about your *underwear*,' Bobbie laughed. 'I meant the dress. Very…sexy…very Liam…'

She was still laughing as she closed the door behind herself.

'Very Liam…' Samantha studied her reflection worriedly. She had noticed, it was true, that James seemed to prefer it when she wore more classically styled clothes, clothes which were elegant and perhaps even a little straitlaced rather than discreetly sexy. Only the previous evening she had seen him frowning over the revealing little tank top which Rosemary had been wearing. Bright cerise in colour, it shouldn't really have suited a redhead, but somehow Rosemary had got away with it—just.

'Do you really think you should be wearing something like that?' James had asked her.

'Why not?' Rosemary had challenged him immediately.

'Well, a woman in your position…' James had responded quietly.

'A woman in my position?' For a moment Rosemary had looked baffled and then she had laughed.

'You mean, because I'm a doctor.'

'No, actually I mean because you're engaged,' James had told her stiffly, quite plainly offended by her laughter.

In reply Rosemary had given him a wide taunting smile.

'It just so happens that my fiancé actually bought me this top,' she told him softly.

'I'll be glad when she finally goes back home,' James had fumed afterwards when they were on their own.

It was on the tip of Samantha's tongue to point out that if he disliked Rosemary's company so much, then the easiest way to avoid having to endure it would be to cut down on his visits to his parents whilst Rosemary was there, but then she reminded herself that she was perhaps being a little unfair. On each occasion they had called round to see them James had done so at his father's behest.

'Officially, of course, he's now retired, but he likes to be kept au fait with what's going on,' James had explained to Samantha.

His concern and consideration for his parents was another indication of the kind of man he was, Samantha recognised.

James, she suspected, would never miss a child's sports day or Christmas play. He would always be there to cheer his children on on the sports field and to listen to their problems.

From speaking to Olivia, Sam had quickly guessed that she would like to add to her family.

'The biological urge runs very strongly through the female side of the Crighton line,' Olivia had told Samantha cheerfully. 'So be warned.'

'I wonder if Maddy's pregnancy will be twins,' Bobbie had mused a little enviously.

'If it is, she isn't saying,' Olivia informed her.

'I can't get over how much Max has changed, can you?'

Olivia and Max had never really got on and Samantha could hear the reluctance in Olivia's voice as she agreed.

'He does certainly seem to have undergone a very dramatic metamorphosis. I must say though that I thought Luke and James were very brave to admit him into their chambers.'

'Luke says it's working out extraordinarily well,' Bobbie had told her. 'In fact, he said the other night that he's actually missing Max and that he's really looking forward to him coming back from holiday.'

'Mmm…well, *he* isn't the only one,' Olivia had responded wryly. 'Uncle Ben has done nothing but complain the whole time Maddy has been away.'

In the renaissance of her marriage Maddy had become pregnant, so family gossip had it, and to her husband Max's proud delight. So many fecund fertile Crighton women. Samantha closed her eyes. When she had confided in Liam her desire for a child, in the depths of her misery and despair, the last thing she had anticipated was that he was going to turn up here in Cheshire.

Damn Liam. Why, oh, why, couldn't he have stayed safely and distantly where he was? And her feelings had nothing whatsoever to do with that sharp sizzling fusion of sexual chemistry she had felt so powerfully when he had kissed her at the airport, Samantha reassured herself— nothing whatsoever.

CHAPTER SEVEN

LIAM thanked the porter and tipped him generously as he showed him up to his suite.

The hotel was fully booked and as he quickly inspected the elegant suite of rooms he had been given he could understand why.

In the bedroom the bed was large and comfortably inviting, the closet space was generous and the bathroom, when he pushed open the door and glanced inside, was equipped not just with a large separate shower but with a huge Victorian-style bath, as well.

His small sitting room possessed a sofa and a large deep chair in addition to a good-sized desk and more than enough power points to satisfy even the busiest of businessmen.

Sarah Jane had enthused over the hotel to him, explaining that it was owned by the Grosvenor family. 'That's the Duke of Westminster,' she had elucidated helpfully whilst Liam's mouth had twitched slightly in amusement.

'Gee, a real live duke,' he had teased her a little, assuming a mock air of disingenuous excitement.

'Louise and Katie had their joint eighteenth birthday party there,' Sarah Jane added. 'Bobbie was there. Joss had invited her. Of course none of the family knew who Bobbie was then and she believed...' She made a small moue.

'*Why* am I telling you all this? You *know* the whole story.'

He did, of course. He knew a lot about Bobbie's tracing her mother's roots.

He had been rather less successful in tracing his own family but he had not really expected anything else.

He had little close family left in Ireland and whilst he suspected if he persevered hard enough, he could no doubt find himself a whole clutch of cousins three and four times removed, it was not really a desire to meet his relatives which had spurred him into crossing the Atlantic.

Common sense told him that the urge, the need, the emotions, which had brought him here were, from a practical point of view, ones he would be best advised to ignore, just as he had forced himself to ignore them on countless previous occasions in the past.

He stood at the window looking down into the busy Saturday mill-race of shoppers and tourists flooding past the hotel and then closed his eyes.

Behind his closed eyelids he could see her so easily. Samantha at fourteen, all gangly legs and braces, her face hot with betraying colour every time she looked at him, tongue-tied and mortified by the extent of her teenage crush on him.

A few weeks later she had unexpectedly and disconcertingly suddenly sprouted a pair of eye-catchingly full breasts, the product so he had discovered, of an illegally purchased well-padded bra.

Sarah Jane had confiscated the garment but it hadn't been all that long afterwards that nature had compensated for this blow to Samantha's teenage ego, only this time the softly rounded curves filling out the front of her T-shirts had had nothing to do with any kind of shop-bought padding. Liam's expert eye had very quickly discerned the difference between the initial rigid protruber-

ences and the much more alluring and distracting little
bounce that the nature-provided pair possessed.

However, with typical female perversity, far from
showing them off Samantha had reacted to their arrival
by taking to wearing huge concealing sloppy-joe tops.

'They embarrass her,' Stephen Miller had confided to
Liam with a mystified male shake of his head. 'Can you
beat that? It's damn near thirty-five degrees out there and
she's wearing a thick fleece sweatshirt. She says the sports
jocks at school stare at her.'

Liam frowned. He could still remember just how that
had made him feel.

The first afternoon he had turned up at the high school
to collect the girls, Bobbie had calmly accepted his ap-
pearance with a grateful smile as he relieved her of her
school books, but Sam had reacted so explosively that
people had turned in the street to look at her.

'I'm not a child,' she had told her parents furiously at
supper that night, ignoring Liam as she glowered over her
meal.

'We were just a bit concerned about you both, hon,'
her mother had palliated. There had been a spate of arti-
cles in the Washington press about diplomats' children
being kidnapped and Sarah Jane had been only too happy
to accept Liam's suggestion that he drive over to the high
school and pick up her daughters.

Predictably, of course, Samantha had retaliated by getting herself a boyfriend—with a car—and announcing that
this spotty, monosyllabic youth would, henceforth, drive
her home.

And so it had gone on and with every twist of the
emotional knife now sunk deep in his guts Liam had
warned himself that what he was doing was wholly and
completely self-destructive; that even if she *had* returned

his feelings, their relationship would be so intense and volatile that it would leave him with no energy for anything else, never mind a politician's career. Sam was too outspoken, too opinionated, too much her own person to be right for him.

In order to accomplish what he wanted to accomplish, in order to go out and do battle and to win in the hostile minefield that was the political arena, when the smallest careless step, the briefest unguarded word could result in one being thrown out of office as carelessly as the Romans had once thrown their Christian prisoners to the lions, having a home life that was a haven of peace and calm, an oasis of sanity, a place as protective of his ego and his self as though it had been his mother's womb, was as vitally essential as breathing oxygen was for life.

And whilst Samantha could be guaranteed to be fiercely protective of her chosen mate and whilst she most certainly would defend him and the children she bore him with every ounce of her skill and fortitude, a calm oasis and a haven of peace she most certainly was not. The relationship; the marriage he had envisaged for himself was one of mutual respect; mutual coexistence, mutual awareness that their relationship was not the motivating prime force of his life. No way would Samantha ever tolerate that!

And yet, she was prepared to marry a man simply because she considered him to be ideal husband and father material. An Englishman who, in her opinion, would prove to be a far better father than her American countrymen.

And who was *he* to try to prove her wrong? Why should he want to? If he had any sense, what he ought to be doing right now was praying for James to marry her just as fast as possible. But when had a man deeply in love ever exhibited any kind of sense?

A man deeply in love!

Liam opened his eyes.

Too many years of loving the wrong woman had quite plainly addled his senses. It must have, otherwise he simply wouldn't be here... So where should he be instead—in Washington with Toni?

Of course, if Samantha *was* determined to marry James then there was nothing he could morally do to stop her, just as there had been nothing he could do to stop her from dating that adolescent high school jerk.

She was, after all, a woman grown and he...

'Oh, what a coincidence,' Bobbie had exclaimed when he had telephoned to tell her that he had booked into the Grosvenor. 'Sam and James are having dinner there together on Saturday night.'

Dinner together and then what? Or were they already lovers? Liam discovered that he had started to grind his teeth. The thought of Sam's magnificent body sensually entwined with that of another man, *any* other man, evoked the kind of primitive reaction inside him that made him want to throw back his head and howl like a hunting wolf. Somehow he didn't think that the Grosvenor would consider him to be a very welcome guest should he attempt to do so.

He glanced at his watch—four o'clock. Bobbie had promised to telephone him in the morning to arrange a get-together. Right now he needed a shower and he could do with something to eat. Picking up the telephone receiver he proceeded to call room service.

*　　*　　*

'Liam's staying at the Grosvenor.' James looked pleased. 'Perhaps we should give him a ring when we get there and invite him to join us for dinner.'

Samantha gritted her teeth. Really, James was just too good-natured and polite at times.

'Oh, but I was looking forward to just *us* having dinner together,' she protested huskily, adding for reinforcement just in case he needed it, 'On our own.'

Was she imagining it or was James deliberately avoiding looking at her?

'Er, well, yes, that would be lovely,' James was agreeing, but his voice wasn't very convincing, Sam recognised a little irritably.

What was the *matter* with him? Initially, when she had arrived in Chester he had seemed thoroughly delighted to see her but these last couple of days she had noticed that, although he was meticulous about keeping to the arrangements they had made, he also seemed to be becoming increasingly distant and preoccupied.

Why...? Surely she hadn't been coming on too strong to him? She had made sure that she wasn't pushing things faster than he wanted to go, but both last night and the night before he had said goodnight to her with little more than a dry-lipped fraternal kiss, even though she had allowed her own lips to part invitingly when he touched them.

'How much longer will Rosemary be staying with your parents?' she asked him conversationally as he drove into the Grosvenor's car park.

'Er... I... I'm not sure...' he replied, adding, 'I hope we can find a car parking spot, otherwise I'm going to have to drop you here whilst I park somewhere else.'

'Mmm... Have you met her fiancé?' Samantha asked him. 'She doesn't seem to mention him very often.'

James was frowning and Samantha heard him curse as

another driver nipped into the only remaining car park spot ahead of him.

'I'll have to drop you here,' he told her curtly, leaning over to unlock the passenger door for her.

'I'll meet you in the foyer just as soon as I've managed to park.'

It was so unlike him to behave irritably that Samantha had felt a little nonplussed. She was aware, of course, that he and Rosemary did not get on but surely her innocent comment about the other girl was not really responsible for his bad temper?

The Grosvenor's foyer was busy and Samantha guessed from the number of smartly dressed people milling around the area that one or more private functions must be taking place.

It was a good fifteen minutes before James finally appeared and he was still frowning Samantha noticed as he made his way towards her and apologised.

'I couldn't find anywhere to park so in the end I drove over to my parents and I've left the car there. We'll have to get a taxi back there to pick up the car.'

His parents—so that explained the touch of lipstick she could just see smudged against his mouth, Samantha acknowledged. Teasingly she pointed it out to him, touched to see the way his colour rose as he took the tissue she was offering him to wipe it off.

It was his mother's of course, and no doubt he was embarrassed at being kissed by her as though he was still a small boy. Tenderly Samantha reached for his hand, intending to give it a little squeeze and to reassure him that she personally found the devotion he had for his parents sweet and touching, but to her chagrin as she did so he moved back from her.

Trying not to feel hurt Samantha allowed him to guide her towards the hotel's main restaurant.

Once they were inside it he gave his name to the maître de and then frowned as he removed Samantha's coat for her.

'I do hope you aren't going to be cold,' he told Samantha pessimistically as he eyed her bare back.

The temptation to whisper throatily to him that if she was she would have to rely on *him* to do something about it died unspoken as Samantha looked into his frowning preoccupied eyes.

James, quite obviously, had something on his mind and even more obviously it was not the same something which was currently on hers. So much for her plans for an evening of seduction, she acknowledged ruefully as the maître de led the way to their table.

Instead of bringing her secret longing for motherhood closer, it seemed instead that it was, in actual fact, receding and becoming even further out of reach.

Bravely refusing to allow herself to get downhearted, Samantha opened the menu the waiter had handed her.

The Grosvenor boasted an innovative and highly acclaimed chef and after Bobbie's descriptions of the wonderful meals she had enjoyed at the hotel, Sam had been looking forward to hers.

James, though, seemed increasingly ill at ease. In an attempt to relax him Samantha asked him if everything was all right.

'Yes, of course, why shouldn't it be?' he responded quickly, too quickly, Samantha felt.

They had just finished their aperitifs and were waiting to give their order when the maître de came over to their table to tell James that there was a phone call for him.

In common with a good many other high-class restaurants, the Grosvenor did not allow mobile phones into the dining room.

Excusing himself to Samantha, James got up and followed the maître de into the foyer where a room was put at the use of guests to take their telephone calls.

When the wine waiter approached the table and asked Samantha if she would like another drink she hesitated and then nodded her head. Perhaps a drink would help her to relax a little bit more; she certainly needed to do so, James' tension was beginning to communicate itself to her.

She had almost finished her drink before he returned looking flushed and anxious.

'What is it? What's wrong?' Samantha asked him solicitously.

'Oh, nothing…it was…it was just a client wanting to know when his case is likely to be heard.'

A *client?* How had he known where to find James? Samantha wondered soberly. She was strongly tempted to accuse James of being less than honest with her but she reasoned with herself, she could be wrong. After all, there was no reason why he should lie to her.

The waiter came and took their order. After the briefest look at the wine list and without consulting her, James ordered the accompanying wine.

That alone was out of character for him. He was normally extremely solicitous about consulting her and almost too fussy about making sure he had chosen a good wine.

The first course came and with it the wine waiter who filled both their glasses.

Samantha had a healthy appetite and enjoyed her food, but watching James pick at his, quite obviously too preoccupied to eat it, destroyed her own desire to eat.

Samantha took a deep breath. Enough was enough. Putting down her cutlery she leaned across the table and began quietly, 'James, something is obviously wrong and…' She stopped, her eye caught by the woman standing in the entrance to the restaurant, a small frown puckering her forehead.

'What is it? What's wrong?' James asked her.

He had his back to the restaurant door but as he saw where Samantha was looking he swivelled round.

Samantha heard the sharp exclamation he made under his breath as he saw Rosemary standing in the doorway.

'James, what…?' Samantha began.

But he was already on his feet, telling her curtly, 'Please wait here, Samantha. I'd better go and see what she wants.'

As he reached the redhead, Samantha saw him take hold of her by her arm and almost march her out into the foyer and beyond her own sight.

The waiter came to ask if they were ready for their main course and Samantha shook her head, instead she allowed the wine waiter to refill her glass.

Sipping on her wine she watched the entrance to the restaurant. Five minutes went by and then ten and then another five. Suddenly Samantha had had enough. Finishing her wine she stood up and, ignoring the enquiring looks of the waiters, she marched purposely towards the foyer.

Initially she was unable to see either James or Rosemary. The foyer was now relatively empty though, certainly empty enough for her to be able to hear their voices coming from the room to one side of the foyer.

Frowning she approached it. By the sound of Rosemary's raised voice, although she couldn't make out *exactly* what she was saying, they were having an argument.

The door to the room was half open. Determinedly, Samantha gave it a push and then gave a small shocked gasp.

Rosemary and James were standing just inside the small room. Rosemary had her back to her whilst James was facing her but he couldn't see her and the reason he couldn't see her was because he was engaged in exchanging an extremely passionate kiss with Rosemary and his eyes were closed. Even so, something must have alerted him to the fact that they weren't alone because, suddenly, he opened his eyes and looked straight at Samantha.

She didn't wait to hear whatever it was he might have to say by way of explanation. What explanation was there, after all, that could serve any useful purpose? She had seen what she had seen and she had certainly seen that James was kissing Rosemary who he purported to dislike intensely, with far more fire and passion than he had ever shown towards her. All right, so they might not be an item; a *couple,* but *that* didn't alter the fact that he had quite deliberately misled her about the true nature of his relationship with the other girl.

Feeling both angry and humiliated Samantha turned on her heel and left, too preoccupied by her own feelings to be aware of the presence of anyone else in the foyer, much less the fact that she was about to cannon into him until the breath was expelled from her lungs with dizzying force and a firm pair of male hands gripped hold of her.

'Liam!' she exclaimed in shock.

'Where's the fire?' Liam joked, and then frowned as he saw her face.

'Sam, what is it? What's wrong...?'

Normally Samantha knew that her pride would never

have allowed her to admit to any kind of failure but she was still in shock from what she had just seen.

'I'll tell you what's wrong,' she told him furiously. '*My* date…the man *I* thought would be the perfect father for my children, is back there smooching with a girl he told me he didn't even like.'

'James is here with someone else.'

Liam looked bemused.

'But I thought *you* were going to be having dinner with him.'

'So did I, but he didn't have much of an appetite for food, nor it seems, for *me* and now I can understand why,' she told Liam bitterly, her eyes filling with dismayed tears which she hurriedly tried to blink away. To have caught James, of all men, in a clinch with another woman when he had… When he had what? When he had *not* wanted her!

A sharp shudder speared through Samantha's body. Perhaps Cliff had been right, after all. Perhaps she *wasn't* the kind of woman…perhaps she wasn't *any* kind of woman enough for a man. Fresh tears smarted her throat.

How *could* James do this to her?

'Liam, what are you doing?' she demanded sharply as she suddenly realised that Liam had guided her towards the lift and had pressed the bell.

'I'm taking you up to my suite so that you can calm down and tell me exactly what's going on.'

'What's going on is that James is a lying perfidious beast who… Oh…' Samantha gave a small soft gasp as the lift arrived and the doors opened, allowing Liam to gently push her into it.

Since several other guests joined them on its upward journey Samantha was unable to protest to Liam that all she really wanted was to be left completely and totally on her own until they were out of the lift and he was guiding her down the carpeted corridor to his hotel room door.

'This isn't any business of yours, Liam,' she told him shortly, 'so please stop trying to interfere… All I want to do is to call a taxi to take me back to Bobbie's.'

'You want to go back to Bobbie, looking like this,' he demanded exasperatedly as he opened the suite door and pushed her in front of the mirror hanging in the tiny entrance lobby.

Whilst Samantha stared in revulsion at her flushed tear-stained face, Liam closed and locked the door behind her.

'Now, come and take a seat, try to calm down and tell me what's happened.'

'What's happened is that James is a lying, cheating rat,' Samantha told him indignantly, refusing to do as he suggested and instead pacing the carpeted floor in front of the suite's sitting room fireplace. The suite, she observed absently, was quite obviously one of the hotel's best ones, lovingly furnished with either genuine antiques or excellent reproductions, the bowl of flowers on one of the console tables was giving off a softly sweet smell but Samantha was in no mood to appreciate the scent of flowers.

'Rosemary is supposed to be engaged to someone else, she's even wearing a ring, and yet just now, downstairs, well, let's just say it was no brotherly kiss he was giving her,' she told him darkly.

Liam's eyebrows rose but initially he made no comment, waiting a few seconds before suggesting calmly, 'Perhaps she's received some kind of bad news and James was comforting her.'

Samantha gave him a scornful look.

'Comforting her? He looked more like he wanted to…' She stopped, her face flushing as she recognised just *what* it was James had looked as though he wanted to do with the woman in his arms.

Samantha closed her eyes, willing the tears she could feel filling her eyes not to fall.

Suddenly she remembered the lipstick that had stained James's mouth when he had returned from parking his car and his earlier preoccupation. Had he and Rosemary...?

'How *could* he do this to me?' she cried, furiously bunching her hands into protesting little fists. 'How *could* he when...'

'Perhaps he didn't realise just what you had in mind for him,' Liam suggested dryly.

Samantha shot him a bitter look.

'He *lied* to me,' she told him fiercely. 'If I had thought for one moment that he was...that there was...

'What's that?' she demanded suddenly, staring at the ice bucket with its complimentary bottle of champagne which was standing on the coffee table.

'Champagne,' Liam told her unnecessarily. 'Look, about James...'

'You haven't opened it yet,' she pointed out.

Liam frowned as he looked at her. Although not a total non-drinker, Samantha had a notoriously low tolerance of alcohol and for that reason tended to avoid anything more than an aperitif followed by a single glass of dinner wine.

'No, I haven't,' he agreed urbanely. 'And if you're suggesting that you'd like a glass... I don't think that would be a good idea.'

'Why not?' Samantha demanded truculently. 'I'm an adult now, Liam, remember, and if I want to get drunk...'
Before Liam could stop her she reached out and removed the bottle from the ice bucket, inexpertly managing to prise the cork free.

The bubbling liquid spilled down over her hands and

when Liam took the bottle from her it ran down his own, as well. Eyeing him challengingly Samantha raised her fingers to her mouth and slowly started to lick the spilt champagne off them.

Liam felt as though someone had hit him good and hard in the solar plexus.

'Cut it out,' he told her sharply.

'Cut what out?' Samantha demanded.

Liam shook his head. Did she *really* not know what she was doing to him, what images she was conjuring up inside his head with her actions? Just watching the way her tongue curled delicately over her fingers made him want to…

'Well, if *you* won't give me a drink then I guess I'm going to have to go down to the bar and buy my own,' Samantha was telling him aggressively.

Liam thought fast.

'Okay…okay,' he told her appeasingly, 'hang on a second whilst I pour it for you.'

With any luck she wouldn't even notice that he hadn't done more than half fill the glass, only it seemed she had and what was more she was letting him know in no uncertain terms that she had.

'Sam, I just don't think this is a good idea on an empty stomach,' he warned as she tilted the glass and drank quickly from it.

'No? Isn't it supposed to be the classic reaction to finding out that you've been betrayed by…' She stopped. She couldn't say by her lover because James wasn't that. 'Not, I suppose, that *you've* ever had to drown the pain that loving someone who doesn't love you back has caused you,' Samantha challenged Liam recklessly.

She was beginning to feel oddly light-headed and reckless, as though someone had taken the brakes off her reactions and emotions. It was a heady, powerful feeling and one she decided she could quite get to enjoy. With James the last few days she had found that she was constantly having to watch her words, to be careful and tactful so that she created the right kind of impression on him, but with Liam, none of that mattered. Liam knew already just what she was like. With Liam she could be as outspoken as she wished, there was no need, no point, in trying to convince *Liam* that she would make good wife material.

'Not in alcohol I haven't,' Liam told her sternly.

'You mean, *you* have loved someone who didn't want you?' Samantha asked him curiously. 'Who?'

'You're going to regret this in the morning,' Liam told her wryly as he recognised the effect the champagne was beginning to have on her.

'Champagne doesn't cause a hangover,' Samantha told him loftily.

Liam looked unimpressed.

'Why was he kissing her when he should have been kissing me?' she demanded mournfully as she eyed the champagne bottle.

'I want another drink, Liam,' she told him plaintively. 'No, don't stop me,' she demanded as he started to shake his head.

'I *need* to get drunk. After all, I'm suffering from a broken heart.'

'Don't be ridiculous, Sam, *you* don't love James,' Liam told her acerbically.

Angrily Samantha tried to focus on him, to tell him just how wrong he was but discovered, to her bemusement, that he was simply refusing to stand still and was, for some reason, swaying from side to side in front of her.

No, of course she didn't love James, but she wasn't going to have *Liam* tell her so.

'Don't I?' she demanded, frowning fiercely at him. 'And just how would *you* know that.'

'For several reasons,' Liam informed her softly, 'all of which I'd be more than happy to discuss with you—when you're sober.'

'I'm sober now.'

'No, you aren't,' he corrected her.

'What reasons? Tell me. I want to know. Tell me, Liam,' Samantha insisted, crossing the floor between them, taking hold of his shirt-clad arm and giving it an angry little shake.

Liam closed his eyes.

This close he could smell the heart-wrenchingly familiar scent of her skin and what was worse, he could feel the way his body was reacting to it and to her. It was just as well, perhaps, that Samantha *was* so tipsy, otherwise she would be able to see just what her presence, her proximity, was doing to him.

'Tell me, Liam,' she was still demanding, her eyes a dark, deep, drownable, fatally alluring heavenly blue. '*What* reasons?'

She was standing so close to him now that— Liam took a deep breath and then another but it was no good, there was no way he could stop what he was feeling.

Almost angrily he took hold of her, pinioning her arms at her side.

'This reason, for one,' he told her grimly as he bent his head and expertly silenced the shocked protest she had been about to make with the firm pressure of his mouth.

Samantha's head was spinning, her thoughts, her reactions, her whole self going crazily out of control. This was Liam who was holding her, *kissing* her, she reminded herself. *Liam* who was just about the nearest thing she had to an elder brother, but her *body* didn't seem to be aware of any barriers her mind was trying to throw up between them. Her *body*... Samantha gave a delicate little shudder as she felt pure female sensual longing pour through her body.

'Mmm...'

Beneath Liam's mouth she made a soft appreciative sound of pleasure and encouragement, lost in the awesome wonder of what she was feeling.

Liam's lips, Liam's tongue, were expertly prising apart *her* closed lips. Dizzily Samantha leant into him.

'Oh, this is pure heaven...'

'Heaven! It's been hell for me,' she thought she heard Liam muttering. 'Wanting you, knowing...'

Liam wanted her!

Bemused Samantha opened her eyes to their widest extent and then closed them quickly again as she realised that Liam's were open and he was looking straight back at her.

Delicious shivers of pleasure were darting all over her body. Why had she *never* realised before now that being kissed could be such a wonderful sensual experience? The hot pressure of Liam's mouth against her own was doing things to her that she never ever wanted to end.

'Don't say that.' She heard Liam groan against her mouth and realised with a small sense of shock that she must have spoken her thoughts out loud.

Dizzily she recognised that she was perhaps not quite as in control of herself as she really ought to be, but somehow it felt like far too much effort to do anything about it and, anyway, why should she want to when she was having such a wonderful, gorgeous, heavenly time in wonderful sexy Liam's arms?

'Mmm... Why have you never kissed me like this before?' she heard herself asking him huskily.

'If you need to ask *that,* then you really have had too much champagne,' Liam responded thickly.

Dreamily she looked up into his eyes.

'Mmm... Liam, *you* are just so sexy,' she breathed happily.

Abruptly he released her.

'Am I? Not five minutes ago you were telling me that you were in love with James. Isn't he the one you should be...'

Samantha glared at him. Not for *anything* was she going to tell him just how disappointed she felt that he had stopped kissing her or just how much she was wishing that he had done more, much, much, more than merely kissed her. If the touch of his lips could make her feel like that, then what would it be like if he were to—

A tiny tremor of excited fear ran down her spine as she recognised the dangerous route her thoughts were taking.

Liam wasn't the man for her. Liam wasn't her kind of man at all. Liam was far too...too...too *much* of a man for *her* liking. What *she* wanted was someone...someone kinder, gentler, someone much *more* malleable. Someone who would not view her with the kind of cynical detachment she was so used to seeing in Liam's eyes when he watched her. Someone, in short, who could not see into her thoughts quite so easily and dangerously as Liam could.

'I really *wanted* to love James,' she told Liam with the mournful honesty of the just-a-little-bit-too-tipsy.

A muscle twitched at the side of Liam's mouth but she couldn't tell whether it was caused by amusement or disgust.

'It's all right for you,' she accused him defensively. 'You…'

'I what?' Liam challenged her.

'It's different for a man.' Samantha backed down a little.

'Not anymore,' Liam advised her wryly.

'Maybe not in theory,' Samantha was forced to agree, 'but in reality…'

She closed her eyes. In reality as she was painfully beginning to learn, a woman was both gifted and cursed by nature in that it was one of her strongest and most powerful basic instincts to nurture and protect the vulnerable life she gave birth to and that instinct went right back to wanting to give that child the very best she could, *even* before he or she had even been conceived. Even the scientists themselves were agreed, women instinctively and automatically picked the mate who would provide their child with the best start in life, which was why *she* had wanted—

But there was no way she could continue with her plans now. Not after she had seen James with Rosemary. Whatever the truth was about their relationship, what Samantha had witnessed had made it overwhelmingly clear to her that there was unfinished business between them and that James was simply not free to father the children she so much longed to have.

'All I wanted was to give my babies the very best father they could have,' Samantha told Liam passionately. 'A father who would put his or her needs first, a father who would be there for them. I don't want my kids to grow up with only their mommy there, with a father whose career is more important to him than his family.

'I've seen what it does to kids to have an ambitious career-orientated father. It's like they're constantly trying

to win his attention—his approval. If *you* ever marry, your
kids will be like that, Liam. Oh, no doubt you'll love
them, in your way, but your work, your career, will always come first...'

'Things are changing,' Liam told her quietly. 'Men *are*
beginning to recognise just what they're missing out
on...'

'Not in Washington they aren't,' Samantha told him
cynically.

She was beginning to feel very tired, oppressed by the
weight of her disappointment. She shivered, wrapping her
arms around her body and closing her eyes as a wave of
physical and emotional exhaustion swamped her.

She had put so much effort into planning her future
with James that now that she was being forced to accept
that her plans were not going to be realised, reaction was
starting to set in, her mercurial temperament causing her
spirits to plummet to the depths of misery and desolation.

All she wanted to do now was to crawl away and hide
herself from the world and everyone in it until she had
had time to come to terms with her disappointment. She
wanted so badly to have a child...children... She had even
mentally pictured their cute little faces, their heads of
thick dark soft hair and their gorgeous grey eyes.
Grey...but James' eyes were brown and... Grey eyes—
like *Liam's!* That was the second time these compelling
grey eyes had intruded on her dreams about future children.

'What's wrong?' Liam demanded sharply as he saw the
way the blood drained from her face as she suddenly
opened her eyes and focused on him.

'Er...nothing...nothing... I just...I'm just so tired,
Liam,' she admitted. 'Everything has gone so wrong...
Why...what is it about me...?' She stopped and shook
her head, fresh tears of self-pity clogging her throat. By

rights she ought to call a taxi and go home to Bobbie's but the thought of facing her sister whilst she was so emotionally upset, of having Bobbie demand to know what was wrong, was just too much for her.

'I...I think I'll call reception and ask them for a room,' she told Liam drearily.

'They're fully booked,' Liam informed her, frowning as he studied her pale face and defeated expression.

In all the years he had known her he had seen her go through many highs and lows, but he had never seen anything affect her as badly as this.

She felt things so fiercely, so passionately, there were no comfortable shades of grey in Samantha's emotional reactions, only blacks and whites.

She hadn't loved James and in losing him she was not losing a lover she was losing a potential father for her children. It was her pride and her belief in her own judgement that was hurting her now, that and her longing for a child, and it was typical of her that she didn't want to be with anyone, even someone as close as her own twin sister.

He glanced through the sitting room of his suite to the closed bedroom door and then looked at Samantha.

'You could always stay here,' he offered.

'Here...in your room.' Samantha frowned. 'But...'

'It isn't a room, it's a *suite,*' Liam pointed out. 'You can sleep in the bedroom, I'll sleep in here on the sofa. It's only for one night, after all...'

He was right, Samantha could see that. The effects of the alcohol she had consumed were wearing off now but she still felt tired and heavy-headed.

'Well, if you're sure you don't mind. Only, *I'll* sleep on the sofa,' she told him firmly, adding, 'It makes much more sense, Liam, after all, you are much bigger than me and it *is* your room.'

Much bigger. How often did she get to say that to a man? Samantha wondered ruefully, but in Liam's case it was true. He was a good few inches taller than her *and* he had the physique to match his height.

It was a mystery to her how he managed to keep so fit given the demands of his career. She knew he played tennis and that he enjoyed walking. Whenever he could he back-packed into the mountains.

'You should try it sometime,' he had teased her once when she had shuddered over the lack of civilised amenities his vacations involved.

'What, without a proper bed or a shower...or anything.' She had grimaced fastidiously. 'No thanks.'

'What do you mean, no showers,' Liam had objected with a wicked glint in his eyes. 'Nature provides some of the best ones there are. Believe me there is nothing but nothing to compare with standing under a cool mountain waterfall and then swimming in a lake so clear that you can see the bottom...'

'Yeah, and having to share it with coyotes and bears and heaven knows what else, as well,' Samantha had objected. 'Like I just said, no thanks.'

'You don't know what you're missing,' Liam had told her softly. 'There's nothing like the cool clean feel of mountain water over naked skin...nothing like cooking out in the open air.'

'Skinny-dipping and barbecues might be your scene but they most definitely are not mine,' Samantha had informed him censoriously.

Liam had still been laughing as she walked away from him, head held high.

She had been much younger then, of course.

Her head was really beginning to ache. Wearily she stifled a jaw-stretching yawn and then a second one.

'Come on. You're exhausted,' Liam told her. 'I guess there'll be some spare bedding in one of the closets, I'll go find it whilst you use the bathroom....'

CHAPTER EIGHT

SAMANTHA woke up and gave a small grunt of pain. The sofa, pretty though it was, had never been designed to be used as a bed and certainly not by a full functioning woman of six foot plus. She winced as she sat up and her contorted muscles howled their protest.

She looked at her watch. She had been asleep for less than two hours.

Now that the alcohol had cleared from her head she was depressingly aware of the failure of her mission.

What were her chances, she wondered, of persuading Saul Crighton to give her a job with Aarlston-Becker thus saving her from the humiliation of having to return home and face Cliff?

She closed her eyes. They felt dry and gritty and her lips, when she touched them with her tongue tip, felt sensitive and faintly swollen—a legacy from Liam's kiss?

That had been such a dangerous thing for her to allow to happen. Now, with her head clear of the effects of the wine and champagne she had drunk she could see just how her behaviour must have looked to Liam. He would have been less than human if he hadn't... If he hadn't what? Taken her to bed? Certainly nothing she had done or said would have given him the impression that she wasn't willing—anything but!

Go to bed with Liam... What a thought... He was the last person... Abruptly Samantha tensed.

Go to bed with Liam... Seduce Liam into giving her a child... Liam, as she already knew, was a very highly

128

sexed man—look at the number of girls he had dated—
and anyway, anyone could see just by looking at him how
sexy he was. With Liam there would be no need to coax
or coerce him into responding; no need to be delicately
guarded or femininely passive. Go to bed with Liam. It
was impossible. Conceive Liam's child... No, she
couldn't, it was totally out of the question, just a mad
thought conjured up by her despair and the loneliness of
the night.

What she was thinking, contemplating, was total and
absolute madness. Was it? Wasn't she, in seducing Liam
into impregnating her, merely following the deepest instinct of her sex? There could be no doubt that genetically
Liam was an A1 choice. He was highly intelligent, physically strong, with the kind of skills that any child would
rejoice in inheriting.

Maybe so, her sterner and more cautious inner self ar-
gued, but he was not a man who could be a father to her
child in all the ways that were so important to her.

Did such a man exist? her other more emotional self
protested. She had thought she had found the perfect husband in James and look how wrong she had been.

But, to have a child outside marriage and by Liam...her
parents...her family... Bobbie would... Never mind her
own strong feelings about shared parenthood.

Did any of them need to know? She could always pretend that the baby, her baby, was the result of a coolly
taken clinical decision and an equally coldly clinical non-
sexual act—an act which she had already vigorously denied to Bobbie that she could ever contemplate. And then
there was Liam himself. But she wouldn't be the first
woman to *choose* to be a single mother.

Liam, with his political ambitions to consider would
probably be only too happy when faced with a fait ac-

compli and her pregnancy confirmed to keep his own role
in her baby's conception a secret, a small inner voice
tempted her dangerously.

No, what she was thinking was totally inconceivable.
Tears filled her eyes. She so much wanted to be a mother.
But, if she was going to pretend to the world that that
was how her child had been conceived then why not do
so, why take the risk of being rejected yet again, of having
Liam turn away from her as James had done?

Why indeed, but in having Liam father her child she
would have the security of knowing just what her baby's
genetic inheritance was. She owed it to her child, too, and
as for Liam rejecting her, well there was only one way
she was going to discover whether or not he would.

In place of the night wear she did not have, she had
wrapped herself in one of the hotel's complimentary tow-
elling robes after having undressed and showered and
now, as she pushed aside the covers on her makeshift bed
and stood up, its soft folds settled warmly around her
body.

He wanted her, Liam had told her earlier, and even
through the fog of alcohol her brain had retained those
words, that admission, and when it came to wanting...

As she walked unsteadily towards the bedroom door
Samantha felt her pulse start to rise and her breathing
become fast and uneven. Perhaps those teenager longings
and desires she had thought so transient had had far
deeper roots than she had imagined and were not quite
dead, after all.

Very gently she opened the bedroom door and walked
into the room. Now that her eyes had accustomed themselves to the darkness she could easily see Liam's sleeping
form on the bed. A quick hot tug of excitement pulled at
her heart, accompanied by a sharp sense of the awesome-

ness of what she was contemplating, but there was no hesitation or reluctance in the way she moved swiftly and softly towards the bed, waiting until she was close enough to lean over him and whisper his name against his lips before she said anything.

At her husky slightly tremulous 'Liam,' Liam woke up instantly, his body tensing, his eyes probing the darkness.

Samantha was leaning over him, her face, her mouth, so close to his that if he breathed a little deeply her lips would be touching his. He had no idea what she wanted but he knew, all too well, what *he* did. His body was making its needs all too urgently clear.

He lifted his arm to switch on the bedside lamp but Samantha stopped him, clasping his forearm and digging her nails a little into his skin in her urgency.

Liam closed his eyes. God, did she have the slightest idea what she was doing to him? He could smell the warm scent of her skin and her robe was so loosely knotted that he could see the full soft swell of her breasts.

The temptation to reach out and push the cloth aside to fully reveal her body, to slide his palm against the heavy fullness of her naked breast and tease the dark burgeoning flesh of her nipple into an aching peak so that she begged for him to take it in his mouth, was so strong that he had to grit his teeth to prevent himself from telling her rawly and explicitly what he wanted to do to her, how he wanted to make her feel…react…need and want him the way he did her. Under the bedclothes his own body was reacting to his thoughts as urgently as though he had actually put them into action.

Swallowing hard, he demanded shortly, 'Sam, what is it…what do you want…?'

He had fed her the perfect line, Samantha recognised. All she needed now was the courage to take it…use it…

Beneath her fingertips the silky hair-covered flesh of his forearm felt so secure and steady. She guessed that, if necessary, it...*he*...could take the whole of her weight and support it... support her, without flinching and certainly without letting her fall...in any way...

The idea of Liam representing any form of security was a novel one and it made her eyes open a little wider in bemused recognition that she was standing on the brink of an unexpected discovery, but there wasn't time to explore such thoughts right now. Right now...

She took a deep breath. Liam was still waiting for her answer. Using her free hand to unfasten the loose tie of her robe, Samantha deliberately slid it free of her shoulders, releasing his arm and leaning ever further towards him as she told him softly, murmuring the words in his ear, 'What I want, Liam, is you...' Then taking her courage in both hands, before he could say or do anything, she turned her head and placed her mouth very delicately and deliberately over his.

For a second the shock of what she was doing held Liam rigid and completely unable to move, but then, almost automatically, he reached out to grasp her shoulders so that he could push her gently away, the strong core of responsibility that was so much a part of his personality overriding the predatory male instincts of his aroused body.

Samantha tensed as she felt his lack of reaction but she was not about to give up now, not without a fight. Reaching out she clasped his face with her hands and proceeded to deepen the intimacy of her kiss, probing the hard shuttered line of his mouth with her tongue, willing him with every ounce of her willpower to respond to her and then, just when she thought she was going to have to give up and admit defeat, she felt the shudder of reaction that ripped through his body, the dry hard heat of the closed line of his lips suddenly giving way as he turned from rejection to responsiveness. Her own body shuddered in relief and then, even more intensely, in almost shocking pleasure as his hands started to knead the tense muscles of her shoulders, his fingers spreading over her skin, massaging and stroking her flesh.

It must be her relief that was making her so responsive to him, Samantha decided dizzily as she twined her arms around him, eagerly opening her mouth to the probing force of his tongue.

He was the one controlling their intimacy now, his hands sliding down her arms and then gripping hold of her as he rolled back onto the bed, lifting the upper half of her body over him as he did so.

Delicious shivers of sensation were washing all through her as his actions brought the full weight of her breasts in tantalising close contact with his bare chest. The soft friction of the silky dark hair that covered it moving against her nipples as he kept on kissing her with ever-increasing intimacy made Samantha long to move closer to him, to press her body against him so that the tormentingly delicate friction became a soothing closeness that would take away the ache flooding through her body. She was lying half on and half off the bed, supported by Liam's hands and totally vulnerable to whatever he chose to do to her, she recognised with a small thrill of sensation which she realised in bemusement was actually excitement.

She was the one supposed to be seducing Liam, she reminded herself severely, and not for the physical satisfaction of having sex with him, but for a more important and serious purpose, a purpose which did not necessitate the kind of long drawn-out sensual foreplay she sensed that Liam was now about to indulge in.

But, for some reason, instead of short-cutting events, Samantha discovered that she was actually encouraging them.

If Liam wanted to tantalise her by only just allowing the aroused peaks of her nipples to brush against the wonderful sensual stimulation of his chest then she guessed she might as well do a little tantalising of her own, perhaps by running her fingertips and then her nails along one smooth hard sloping shoulder, just oh, so lightly raking the skin there.

As she felt him shudder in response, Samantha smiled secretly to herself. His lower body and hers might be separated by the thickness of the bedclothes but her woman's instinct told her that he wanted her.

A glorious sense of triumph and happiness filled her, a sense of strength and power, of freedom to be completely and totally herself. Joy bubbled up inside her and along with it a soft gurgle of laughter.

'What's funny?' Liam demanded as he heard it.

'Nothing,' Samantha whispered back honestly against his mouth, lifting her head to rub her face tenderly against his as she told him, 'I just feel *so* good…so…so *happy*…'

As he heard what she was saying Liam veiled his eyes with his eyelashes. Had she *any* idea just what she was saying to him? If *he* had any sense he would stop this right now before it got any further.

'Liam…'

In his hold, Samantha gave a small wriggle of impatience and then determinedly caressed his throat with her mouth, lingering deliberately over the hard swell of his Adam's apple until she felt him swallow in reaction to the sensuality of what she was doing. The words of soft

denial he had been about to utter were lost, drowned out
by the groan of longing that thundered in his chest. His
hands slid from her arms to her breasts as he caressed
them as he had imagined doing not just once, but a thousand, no a hundred thousand times in the years since she
had reached maturity.

Lifting her further above him, he caressed the smooth
warm swell of her breast with his mouth and then opened
it over the dark ripe temptation of her nipple.

Samantha moaned sharply out loud as her body reacted
to the swift suckling movement of his mouth, with a surge
of pleasure so intense that it shocked her.

Her nails raked the warm flesh of Liam's arms. Her
hips writhing frustratedly against the thick muffling barrier of the bedclothes.

'Liam, Liam…' She tugged impatiently on his hair,
shuddering as explosions of pleasure racked her body
when he continued to caress her breasts. It was like being
lapped by an inner tide of feeling, a tide which grew increasingly strong with every surge it made, a tide whose
swift undercurrents she could already feel tugging deeper
and deeper at the most private core of her being.

'Liam.'

Frantically she pulled at the bedclothes, desperate to
wrench them away so that she could get closer to his
body, to the wonderful maleness of him, to the comple-
tion, the satisfaction, the *oneness* her body craved and
which she knew instinctively only his could soothe and
satisfy.

Logical reasoning had long since been abandoned. She
was operating on instinct alone now, driven and possessed
by it and by her need—a need that only Liam could satisfy.

'I want you… I want you… I want you so much, Liam,'

she told him, frantically whispering the words against his
hair, his throat, just any part of him she could reach out
for and touch. When she felt him rolling her over onto
the bed beside him she reached towards the bedclothes,
fiercely pushing them out of the way, her fingers meshing
with Liam's as he did the same thing. Her eyes attuned
fully now to the darkness quickly picked out the shape of
his naked body as he pushed aside the duvet. Sharply she
drew in her breath.

Watching her, Liam reflected that a man would have to
be a saint not to react to the look he could see gleaming
in her eyes as she studied him, so totally absorbed in
visually drinking in every detail of him that she reminded
him of a child unwrapping her Christmas presents.

Without the slightest hint of self-consciousness she
reached out and traced the length of his arm, her eyes
never leaving his body as she explored the flatness of his
belly, but then as her fingertips touched the thick darkness
of his male body hair she suddenly tensed and raised her
gaze to his.

'What is it?' he asked her gruffly.

Samantha looked at him, her face slightly flushed.

'You're just so *beautiful*,' she told him softly. She
could see the way his whole body shook with laughter.

'*I'm* beautiful…!'

Still laughing he reached up and took hold of her.

'I'll show you what's beautiful,' he told her huskily.
'This is beautiful.' He kissed one nipple slowly and tenderly. 'And this…'

Samantha trembled as he kissed the other one oh, so
lingeringly.

'…And this…' His mouth was caressing the soft
warmth of her belly. 'And these…'

He reached down and stroked his hands up over her

knees and along her thighs and Samantha made a soft anguished sound of tormented pleasure.

'And this...'

All the breath in her lungs wheezed out of her in shock as Liam turned her on her back and slipped between her legs, his fingers gently probing the secret of her sex, his mouth slowly caressing it.

The undercurrent to the tide she had felt earlier had now become an inescapable force that threatened to swamp and flood her.

'*You* are beautiful...more beautiful than any woman has any right to be, more beautiful than any other woman could ever possibly be,' she heard Liam telling her thickly as he slowly gathered her up in his arms and covered her with his body.

As he wrapped his arms around her and kissed her, Samantha was conscious of only one thing and that was her need to complete the magical cycle that they had begun, but as she moved to wrap her legs around him, Liam moved his body away from her, kissing her briefly as he whispered, 'Stay there...'

'Stay there!' Confused Samantha watched in disbelief as he got off the bed and padded towards the bathroom. Her whole body was on fire for him, aching for him, so much so that she was actually beginning to shiver as pitifully as a drug addict caught up in the agony of deprivation because he wasn't there.

In the bathroom Liam searched feverishly through the basket of complimentary toiletries for the discreet package he had seen tucked there earlier. The hotel, it seemed, intended to make sure that their guests practised safe sex, which was just as well because his current lifestyle certainly did not include carrying the means for doing so around himself.

Samantha was lying still, curled up in a bundle of rejection, her eyes closed against her pain—why had he disappeared, left her like that?—when he returned.

'Liam,' she began shakily as he touched her and then stopped as he wrapped her in his arms and proceeded to kiss her whispering, 'Sorry, something I had to do.'

Her relief at his return and at the fact that he still wanted her prevented her from asking a question. Her body already aching with longing for him quickly caught fire from the hungry caress of his hands and this time it was Liam who moaned out loud as he held her hips and she arched her body towards his in invitation and abandonment.

As he entered her, Liam felt the universe turn full circle around him. They fitted together so well they might have been made for one another. He could feel her body responding to every movement of his own, welcoming each powerful thrust, caressing and holding him so lovingly that he could feel his eyes smarting with tears of emotion.

Samantha's eyes were starting to burn with her own shocked, emotional tears. Nothing had prepared her for the intensity of what she was experiencing and it wasn't just the sensation of Liam's body drawing hers to the edge of the precipice which would ultimately throw them both over to free fall through time and space as though they were immortal, that was arousing her almost too unbearably. No, it was the sure strong knowledge that this was her destiny and Liam her mate—that being with him like this now was the most powerful pivotal moment of her whole life.

'Mmm...' Lazily, her eyes still closed, Samantha reached out for the wonderful male warmth she had sensed had been there beside her in bed whilst she slept. But it *wasn't* there any longer. Anxiously she opened her eyes and then as she came fully awake her awareness of what had happened the night before brought her bolt upright in bed, panic, disbelief and denial all clamouring for supremacy in her overloaded brain.

Vaguely she was aware of another external noise overriding the frantic buzzing of her confused thoughts. Someone was knocking on the outer door of the hotel suite.

The bathroom door opened and Liam strode into the room, his hair wet, a towel wrapped discreetly around his hips.

'Mmm…good morning,' he murmured, coming over to the bed and leaning down, obviously intending to kiss her. Nervously Samantha leaned out of the way.

'The door, Liam,' she told him.

'It must be the waiter with our breakfast,' he told her, adding throatily, 'I don't know about you but I sure worked up an appetite doing *something* or other last night!'

Silently Samantha watched him walk into the suite's sitting room. Last night she had seduced Liam into making love to her—not that he had needed much persuasion, she defended herself quickly.

How *could* she have done such a thing? She closed her eyes. She knew only too well how… How many, many times in the past had she cursed the impetuosity of her volatile nature, the need for action, which sometimes overrode all the cannons of common sense and caution. She had done some mighty foolish things in the past, but *nothing,* not one single one of them had come *anywhere near* beating the magnitude of the folly she had committed last night.

Lost in the painful mental interrogations she was subjecting herself to she was only vaguely aware of Liam answering the impatient summons to open the suite door.

But it *wasn't* the waiter with the breakfast he had ordered he was admitting to his suite, Samantha recognised with a sharp thrill of horror, it was Bobbie and her mother-in-law Pat.

'Oh, Liam, thank goodness you're here,' she heard Bobbie exclaiming worriedly. 'You haven't seen anything of Sam, have you? She never came home last night. She and James were to have dinner here at the Grosvenor and, at first, when she didn't come back I thought... But then when James rang this morning asking for her—'

As she heard her sister's voice becoming clearer and clearer, Samantha stared transfixed at the bedroom door which Liam had left partially open. Perhaps if she moved now she might just make it to the bathroom where she could conceal herself, but even as she frantically wondered what to do she heard her twin's sharp in-drawn breath of shock as she came into view standing in the open bedroom doorway staring stupefied at her.

'Samantha...' she breathed jerkily, whirling round to look pink-faced at Liam exclaiming, 'Oh Liam, I...'

'Bobbie, I can explain,' Samantha called out protestingly but her sister was already discreetly hurrying her mother-in-law away from the open bedroom door. Samantha could hear her apologising to Liam, explaining, 'Liam, I'm so sorry, I had no idea...no one, *Samantha* never said...but I suppose I should have guessed. The two of you always did strike sparks off one another... Oh, but the folks will be so pleased.'

Bobbie's shock was quite obviously giving way to excitement and suddenly she reappeared in the open doorway calling out to Samantha, 'Sam, I'm going to give the both of you one hour to get yourselves downstairs so that we can all celebrate. Fancy not even giving *me* a hint. Oh, my…just wait until I tell Luke…'

'Bobbie. *No*. You don't understand,' Samantha started to protest in panic but her twin was already ushering her bemused mother-in-law towards the suite door.

'Liam, I *am* sorry if we appeared at an inappropriate moment.' She could hear Bobbie laughing. 'But you really have only yourselves to blame. I know what it's like when you're freshly in love and you just want to keep the whole thing to yourselves, but Sam might have given me some kind of hint. And to think that *I'd* almost got her paired off with James.

'Well, Luke is quite definitely going to say "I told you so" to me. He's maintained all along that Sam and James would never suit…and Pat is convinced—' She broke off, giving Pat a rueful smile before her mother-in-law tactfully left, and then turned back exclaiming, 'Oh, Liam…'

In the hallway to the suite Bobbie flung her arms excitedly around Liam and hugged him.

'I am just *so* pleased for you both. I know that Sam has always maintained that she was over her teenage crush on you but I've always had my doubts—and who can blame her. If I didn't love Luke so much…' Bobbie laughed and hugged Liam a second time. 'Oh, I can't wait for Mom and Dad to come over now. This family is just going to have so much to celebrate—Pop's retirement, your inauguration *and* a wedding…'

As she heard the suite door close behind her sister, Samantha slid down beneath the bedclothes, hugging them protectively around her.

As soon as Liam appeared in the still open doorway she demanded accusingly, '*Why* did you let her in…?'

'I didn't have much choice,' Liam retorted calmly, 'and besides…'

'…and why didn't you tell her the truth?' Samantha shrilled furiously at him. 'Why did you let her go on and on like that about us being a couple…in love…? Now she thinks that we're about to get married and…'

'Is that such a bad idea,' Liam interrupted her quietly, quickly seizing the opportunity fate had so unexpectedly given him.

Samantha stared at him. She *had* to be hearing things.

'Us…get married…you and me…' She started to shake her head and then stopped as the appalling truth hit her.

'You *planned* this, didn't you,' she accused him in a shocked whisper. 'You *planned* it. You *deliberately*…' She closed her eyes and gulped. 'Oh, but I've been such a fool,' she told him angrily. 'I can see it all now… Miss Washington PR turned you down and so you targeted *me*. After all, what better wife *could* you have than the daughter of the retiring Governor… I'm the perfect wife, for you aren't I, Liam…and more importantly, my father is the perfect father-in-law… Oh…'

'What the hell are you saying?' Liam interrupted her sharply, his original rush of exhilaration turning swiftly to angry pain. 'You've got to be joking.' But he could see from her face that she wasn't and that she honestly believed the accusations she was hurling at him. He had expected her to be slightly withdrawn from him this morning, to feel a little shy and hesitant, but this… Of course it was unfortunate that Bobbie had seen Samantha in his bed and jumped to the natural conclusion, but…the very idea that Sam could honestly believe that he would stoop so low as to deliberately trick her into a compromising position was so crazy that he ought to be laughing at her, but he couldn't. The way she was reacting rubbed raw against his pride…and against his heart. He had genuinely thought that last night could be the start of—of what?

He had been a fool to let his hopes get out of hand like that and even more of a fool to let his needs get even further out of hand.

Samantha was throwing back the bedclothes and scrambling for the robe she had discarded the night before.

'I need to speak to Bobbie…' she was telling him frantically, almost gabbling the words in her fury. 'I need to tell her the truth…'

'The truth…'

Liam could feel his own anger rising to match hers. 'And just *what* exactly might that be?' he demanded bitingly, his eyes turning an ominous shade of dark stormy grey.

'What are you going to tell her Sam…? Are you going to tell her how you crawled into my bed and begged me…'

'No.'

Angrily Samantha placed her hands over her ears to shut out his shaming words.

'No?' In two strides Liam was across the floor, wrenching her hands away from her ears.

'*You* can tell Bobbie what lies you choose, Sam, and I can't stop you, but the truth is that last night you wanted me…you begged me…you…'

'I *wanted* to get pregnant,' Samantha railed back at him, her face hot with the intensity of her emotions. 'I *wanted* you to give me a child.'

Immediately Liam released her hands and stood back from her. His face had gone white, his jaw clenched tight. Samantha had never ever seen him looking so angry and for a moment she felt almost afraid of him, shivering as she anticipated the cruelly destructive lash of his tongue as he lacerated her pride with his condemnation of her, but instead, as he turned his back on her and stared out of the window he was motionless and silent for so long that Samantha didn't know how to react. Her own shock-induced anger was beginning to ebb away, now leaving her feeling both ashamed and vulnerable. It was her own sense of shame at being discovered in his bed by her twin that had led her to react so horribly to him. She knew that she owed him an apology.

And then, just when she thought he simply wasn't going to speak to her at all, he began to do so but so quietly that she had to strain her ears to catch what he was saying.

'For your information,' he told her with his back still to her, 'the reason, the only reason, I didn't correct Bobbie's misunderstanding of the situation was because *I* wanted to protect *you*—and not just you, Sam, but your family, as well. Do you really think if I wanted a wife so badly, that I couldn't find one?' he challenged her as he swung round, adding in savage indictment, 'And I'd sure as hell have to be desperate to pick you, despite what you seem to think.

'I can't *think* of a single woman out of all the women I know who is *less* emotionally and mentally equipped to take on the role of Governor's wife. You epitomise every characteristic that no politician in his right mind wants in a partner. You're impulsive, you leap to implausible conclusions and, even worse, you act on them as though they're known facts. You're stubborn to the point of totally illogical wrong-headedness, you won't listen to reason, you...'

To her chagrin Samantha discovered that tears were pouring down her face.

'...and as for what you said about going to bed with me so that you could get pregnant...'

To Samantha's shock he threw back his head and laughed harshly.

'What is it? What's so funny?' she demanded. 'Why are you laughing?'

'I'm laughing my dear, dear Samantha, because if you'd told me at the start just why you wanted to go to bed with me, there's no way you'd have ever got me there, and if you don't believe me then try asking yourself just why I took the trouble to make sure that you were protected—to make sure that there *were* no consequences...'

'"No consequences,"' Samantha repeated dully. She stared at him her anger rising again. '*No* consequences...' She thumped the bed in furious indignation. '*My* baby is not a *consequence,* I'll have you know, Liam Connolly. *My* baby...'

'*Our* baby,' Liam corrected her grittily. '*Our* baby, that's what he or she would have been, Sam. Not *your* baby but *ours* and there's no way I'd ever allow my child to be brought up by a woman who's got the kind of half-baked ideas that you...'

They were off again, arguing, accusing and counter-accusing whilst Samantha struggled to take in what he had told her. That visit to the bathroom which she had dismissed merely as a frustrating interruption of their love-making had had a purpose she hadn't even guessed at.

'I hate you,' she told him passionately as her eyes clouded with fresh tears.

'I don't feel too hot about you, either, right now,' Liam told her grimly, 'but that still doesn't alter the fact that in less than an hour's time you and I are going to have to put on a convincing show of being idyllically in love.'

'What!' Samantha's jaw dropped.

'You heard me,' Liam told her curtly. 'Right now your sister believes that you and I, having spent an illicit night of passion in one another's arms, are about to swear eternal love to one another.'

'I'm going to tell her the truth,' Samantha reminded him shakily.

'Are you?' Liam shook his head. 'I don't think so,' he told her firmly. 'Have you thought about what this could do to your parents, Samantha? How they're going to feel knowing that you took me to bed purely to get yourself pregnant.'

Samantha opened her mouth and then closed it again.

'I... I won't tell them about that. I'll say it was just...just...'

'Just what? A moment of passion, and have them think that *I* seduced their daughter. Oh, no. No way are you going to put me in that kind of bind,' Liam told her softly. 'Oh, no, right now the only way you and I have of getting out of this with our reputations intact is to play along with Bobbie's belief that we're deeply in love and truly a committed couple.'

Deeply in love...*committed. Her* and *Liam*... Samantha opened her mouth to object to what he was saying and then closed it.

'Yes,' Liam challenged her tersely. '*If* you've got another solution then I'd sure like to hear it.'

Dumbly, Samantha shook her head. His mention of her parents had brought her sharply and painfully down to earth. She knew just how shocked and upset they would be if they heard the truth, how hurt and saddened by her behaviour—and Liam's. They already thought of Liam almost as a son and the news that he was to be their son-in-law would delight *both* her parents, but most especially her father.

'But I can't marry you,' she whispered painfully. 'You're going to be Governor and I don't... I can't...'

'Who said anything about *marriage?*' Liam derided her.

Uncertainly she looked at him.

'All I'm saying is that for now, for *everyone's* sake, you and I have to play along with Bobbie's assumptions and allow everyone to believe that we're in love and planning to get married.'

'But we aren't *going* to get married,' Samantha repeated, keeping her gaze fixed on Liam's face.

Immediately he shook his head.

'Oh, no. No way,' he told her savagely. 'No way would I ever marry a woman who only wanted me for the children I could give her.' He looked at his watch.

'We've got half an hour to get downstairs, unless of course you want your sister to think we're so passionately in love that we've gone back to bed, that we simply *can't* keep our hands off one another.'

Flinging him an indignant look, Samantha immediately hurried towards the bathroom. How *dare* he suggest anything of the kind. Just because last night she had seemed to...to want him... She had already told him the reason for *that.*

Once inside the bathroom with the door locked safely between them, Samantha tossed her head indignantly. *Her* want Liam... That was ridiculous...totally and absolutely ridiculous...wasn't it? And the minute she had Bobbie to herself she was going to tell her.

With the water from the shower cascading noisily behind her, Sam bit her lip. She was going to tell Bobbie what? That she and Liam had... She gave a small hurting swallow, the words 'had sex' almost physically hurting her as she tried to force herself to frame them mentally and discovered that, for some reason, the words she actually wanted to use were 'made love.'

But she and Liam had *not* made love. How could they when they did not love one another, when Liam did not love her?

Sam could feel shock zigzagging down her spine in sharp ice-cold splinters of pain just like the ones that were embedding themselves in her heart.

Tears welled up in her eyes. Angrily she blinked them away. What she was crying for was simply the loss of her childhood ideals, her belief that only within the loving intimacy of a committed relationship could she truly experience the physical fulfilment she had had with Liam last night, that only with a man she loved utterly and totally could she want to conceive a child... *his* child.

What had happened to her and to those beliefs that she had been willing to trample on them and to ignore them?

She *deserved* to be in the situation she now found herself in, she told herself uncompromisingly.

As she stepped into the shower, her mouth twisted in a small sadly wry smile. Well, at least no one who knew them was likely to be too surprised when she and Liam decided that their relationship wasn't going to work and that they wanted to go their separate ways.

And there was another aspect to the situation which Liam had not mentioned but which she was uncomfortably aware of.

Whilst Bobbie got on very well with her in-laws, Sam knew that her own mother had always felt a little bit uncomfortable with people because of the circumstances surrounding her own birth.

In the Crighton family, Ruth was treated with the respect she thoroughly deserved and even the realisation by other members of her family that she had borne the illegitimate daughter of her wartime lover and then been forced by her family to give up that baby for adoption had not changed her family's love or admiration for her. And nor, of course, should it have done. The story of Ruth's love for Grant and the trauma of her having to give up their daughter, Sarah Jane, was an extremely harrowing one, but now the whole family was reunited, Ruth and Grant were married, but still their daughter had never totally overcome her insecurity about being harshly judged by others because of the circumstances of her birth.

Her mother, Sam knew, would be very upset to think that Patricia Crighton had seen Sam in a compromising situation with Liam and might in consequence judge her daughter poorly.

No, for her mother's sake as much as anything else Sam knew that she had to go along with Liam's suggestion— go along with, maybe, but if Liam thought for one moment that she was about to be *grateful* to him for doing the gentlemanly thing...

Angrily Sam stepped out of the shower and started to vigorously towel herself dry.

She had just about finished when she heard a firm rap on the bathroom door.

'I'm nearly through,' she called out curtly to Liam.

'Open the door, Sam,' she heard him demanding, ignoring her response to his knock.

Pulling on her robe she opened the door and told him waspishly, 'There, I've finished and...'

She had stopped abruptly as she saw the parcels Liam was carrying and started to frown, 'You've been out to the stores, but...'

'Trousers and a top,' he told her laconically, handing over two of the shiny bags to her. 'I think I've got the size right...'

Sam stared at him, eyes widening.

'I didn't think you'd want to meet with everyone wearing the same dress you had on last night.'

He was right of course, that had been a strictly-for-a-sexy-date dress and was hardly suitable for a family lunch. Even so, for some reason, the knowledge that Liam had actually taken the trouble to go out and shop for her was making her feel not just surprised but ridiculously over-emotional.

She could feel the tears starting to burn her eyes and in an effort to conceal them from him she lowered her head over the bags and told him grumpily, 'They probably won't fit.'

'Try them,' Liam advised her coolly.

Leaving the bathroom free for him, Samantha hurried into the bedroom.

Inside the larger carrier was a small one which she opened curiously before removing the tissue-packed trousers it contained. Inside the small carrier, also tissue wrapped, was exactly the kind of elegant plain underwear she normally favoured. Even the colour of the semi-nude bra and briefs was exactly the shade *she* would have chosen and she realised with a small sense of shock the size was exactly right, as well.

Now, how on earth had Liam known that? Either he had made a very inspired guess or he knew her much better than she thought. At a pinch, she guessed, she could have shopped for him and got everything in the right size but men were notorious for getting underwear measurements wrong. This bra he had bought for her was exactly right and the briefs were even in the style she favoured for wearing under trousers.

Quickly checking that the shower was still running she closed the bedroom door and slipped them on. She had been feeling rather unhappy about the idea of donning last night's worn things—one of the virtues or vices, depending on how you looked at it, of inheriting half of your genes from a strictly traditional New England family was a near obsession with cleanliness.

A little curiously she removed the trousers Liam had bought for her from their tissue wrapping. From the carrier bag she knew he had bought them from an extremely expensive local store and the label on the caramel-coloured fine wool pants confirmed their quality—Ralph Lauren no less—and as she held them up in front of her Sam knew that they would be a perfect fit.

Like the cream silk shirt he had bought her to go with them and the suede loafers she found in the third bag, everything was so very much in her own style that she could quite easily have bought them herself.

When she turned up downstairs wearing these clothes, Bobbie would automatically assume that she had.

She had just finished brushing her hair when Liam returned to the bedroom, one eyebrow raised as he asked her questioningly, 'Everything okay?'

'They fit fine,' Sam agreed grudgingly, and then her natural sense of fair play and honesty forced her to add, 'They're exactly what I would have chosen for myself. You'll have to give me the bills for them.'

'There's something else,' Liam told her, ignoring the latter part of what she was saying and going over to the coffee table in the suite's sitting room to pick up a small bag Sam had not noticed before.

'I guess if we're going to do this, we'd better go all the way,' he told her mystifyingly as he opened the small shiny dark green bag and removed an even smaller square jeweller's box.

Samantha's heart gave a shocked-bound thudding against her chest wall.

Liam had bought her jewellery…a ring?

'Give me your hand,' she heard him demanding calmly.

Her mouth had gone too dry for her to be able to utter the denial she wanted to make but her whole body trembled as Liam took hold of her left hand, giving her a slightly grim look as he warned her, 'This is no time to start being dramatic, Samantha. You can be sure that right now, whoever is downstairs is expecting us to emerge as a blissfully happily committed couple.'

'No,' she denied quickly. 'Why should they? Bobbie won't have said anything…'

Liam's eyebrows lifted.

'Maybe not in normal circumstances,' he agreed, 'but she wasn't on her own when she saw us. She had Pat with her,' he reminded Samantha, and although he didn't want to provoke another row with Sam he had seen the look of relief in Bobbie's eyes when neither of them had denied their love for one another.

James' parents, whilst welcoming Bobbie to their family were a slightly old-fashioned and very traditional couple. Neither of James' sisters had lived with their now husbands before their marriages and both of them had lived at home whilst attending university in Manchester. Even though it was over an hour's drive away, and whilst there was no way that he was dependent on Sam's father's goodwill to further his political career, he liked the older man far too much to want to cause him any embarrassment or pain— A mutually broken off engagement would be far easier for Sam's parents to accept than a mere one-night stand—not that he ever had any intentions—but his intention, his hopes and needs, had to be put on hold right now, especially with Sam reacting as she was doing.

Concentrating on digesting the unpalatable truth of what Liam was saying, Samantha did not at first pay much attention to the ring he was removing from its box until the white flash of diamonds not so much caught as regally demanded her attention.

When she did look at the ring he was coolly slipping onto her finger she couldn't prevent herself from giving a stunned betraying gasp.

The central flawless sapphire was the deepest densest blue she had ever seen and just about as close to the colour of her own eyes as it could possibly be, whilst the diamonds which surrounded it were sharply white, perfectly clear glittering stones.

It was, Samantha recognised, the kind of ring any woman would be thrilled to receive. Surely only a man deeply in love would choose a stone that so exactly matched his adored one's own eye colour and he would certainly have to be totally besotted to spend the amount of money Samantha guessed *this* ring must have cost Liam.

'What did you do,' she joked shakily, 'hire it for the day...'

The look of hauteur Liam gave her made her feel even more shaky.

'Liam, it's...it's...' She shook her head, unable to find the words to tell him what she thought of his quixotic impulse. 'It must have been so expensive,' she told him weakly. 'What on earth will you do with it...afterwards...'

'Concern—for me?—*that* must be a first,' Liam told her dryly as he closed the box with a firmly businesslike air.

'Hopefully in the fuss over our "engagement" surprise, the way in which our relationship was exposed to the light of day will be overlooked,' he told her sardonically.

'Engaged.' Samantha shook her head. 'But Mom and Dad...'

'...will understand when I explain that it was only the discovery of how much I was missing you and what I stood to lose that prompted me to act impetuously and rush over here to propose to you,' Liam told her calmly.

'Lovers seldom act rationally...so why should we be any exception? I proposed, you accepted, and of course, I couldn't wait to show the world that you're mine by waiting until we got home to get you a ring. After all, it isn't as though I have your ability to trace my family back to the Pilgrim Fathers and beyond and there are certainly no family heirlooms waiting in bank vaults to be handed over to my wife-to-be,' he told her grimly.

Samantha gave a thoughtful look. She knew of Liam's family history and how, as immigrants, they had arrived in America with virtually nothing, but his words brought home to her again how sensitive Liam felt about the subject.

'You can't think that if I were in love it would matter to *me* who my partner's antecedents were,' she challenged him.

'No, but surely you'd want to know what kind of genes you were passing on to your kids, wouldn't you?'

'If I loved someone then I would want my child—our child—to have his genes,' she reiterated firmly.

Liam gave her a cynical smile.

'Well, let's hope the voters "love" *me* enough to overlook my lesser heritage,' he told her wryly.

Samantha frowned. 'You don't honestly think that people would be put off voting for you because of that?' she demanded before telling him passionately, 'It's obvious that you're the best man for the job, Liam, and any voter who can't see that for themselves doesn't, in my view, deserve to be allowed to vote.'

'Very democratic,' Liam told her, his expression lightening to one of rueful amusement. 'You really are an all-or-nothing person, Sam, you either love or hate, there's no halfway house with you, no middle ground.'

'Just because I have strong beliefs, that doesn't mean that I can't see another person's point of view,' Samantha objected. 'I'm not intolerant, Liam.'

'No, just passionately opposed to anyone who doesn't share your point of view,' Liam responded with another smile, glancing at his watch and then warning her, 'Come on, we'd better go down and face the music.'

CHAPTER NINE

'COME on, in you go.'

'Oh!'

Samantha gave a small exclamation of stunned disbelief as Bobbie, who had been waiting for them in the hotel foyer, gave her a little push and stood to one side in the open doorway of the hotel's private function room.

Instead of half a dozen or less people Samantha had expected to see, the room seemed full of a sea of expectant faces. For a moment she was tempted to turn tail and run but as though he knew how overwhelmed she felt Liam stepped up behind her, his arm curling supportively around her as he drawled to Bobbie, 'Seems like someone's been busy...'

Samantha heard Bobbie laugh, her initial panic subsiding as she realised that in truth the room only held a relatively small proportion of their many relatives, around a dozen or so, all of them smiling at her in loving happiness and expectancy.

'Well, I just *had* to ring Jenny to give her the news because I knew that she'd already arranged a family lunch here today because Katie's at home and she'd invited Max and Maddy to join them with the children and so I said why didn't we all have lunch together. You don't mind do you?' she asked Samantha. 'Only I'm just so excited for you, Sam. It's like a romance story come true, you falling for Liam in such a big way all those years ago, worshipping him from a distance and having the biggest crush in the world on him,' she teased. 'And now, all these years later the two of you falling for one another as equals. And now,' she added expressively rolling her eyes as she gave them both a merry look, 'Liam must love you to pieces to have followed you right across the Atlantic. She'll make the world's worst Governor's wife, Liam,' she added warningly.

'Oh, thanks,' Samantha told her twin grimly.

'It's true,' Bobbie laughed. 'The first time there's a march outside government house you'll be the one leading it. Do you remember when she organised that protest march against hunting, Liam?' she asked him.

'Will I ever forget it,' Liam responded ruefully. '*I* was the one who had to go get her released from the police cells...'

'Yes, and you were the one who, when we got home, told me I'd have to shower in the backyard just in case I'd picked up...something...' Samantha gave a deep shudder at the memory his words had evoked. Perhaps it was true that she *had* reacted rather recklessly and dangerously, but surely Liam had *over*reacted in his furious cold anger to her when he had come to bail her, cruelly telling her that some of her co-marchers may not be too particular about their personal hygiene.

Whether or not he had been right had never been proved. It had been enough that she had spent the whole night lying awake wondering if every tiny little scalp itch was the forerunner of some unpleasant and unwanted cohabiters.

First thing in the morning she had taken herself off to the hairdressers where she had had her long hair cropped.

She could still remember how her mother had cried when she had seen her and she could remember, too, the look of cold disgust in Liam's eyes as he studied her boyishly barbered short hair. She had grown it long again, but now preferred her hair cropped although in a much more feminine version of her original cut.

'That was when you had your hair cut,' Bobbie added, almost as though twin-fashion, she had followed Samantha's own train of thought.

'Do you remember, Liam?' she asked. 'Poor Mom cried.'

'Yes,' Liam said. 'I remember.'

How terse and angry Liam sounded. Samantha turned her head to look at him and then stood completely still in the circle of his arm, their onlookers forgotten as she saw the look in his eyes.

'Your lovely hair... I didn't know whether to throttle you or...' Liam was telling her softly. 'Not that it didn't suit you short then or now...'

Suspecting that he was trying to sound diplomatic and lover-like because Bobbie was listening Samantha was just about to try to reply in a way that was equally pseudo lover-like when, to her disbelief she heard Bobbie chiming in, 'Oh, yes, I can still remember how chagrined I felt a while back when I overheard Liam telling someone that he thought your cropped curls were just the most alluringly sexy tease on a woman with such a sensationally curvy body.'

Her eyes rounding, Samantha stared at him.

'You said *that*,' she questioned faintly, 'about *me*...'

'I suppose I should have guessed then,' Bobbie was saying as she determinedly ushered them into the Grosvenor's private function room and called out to the assembled throng, 'Here they are everyone. The Crighton family's latest formally accredited "couple."'

Out of nowhere a waiter suddenly appeared circulating the room with trays of bubbling champagne, or so it seemed to Samantha as she and Liam were engulfed by the excited and enthusiastic members of her family who were waiting to congratulate them.

'I thought you said just a quiet family lunch,' Samantha complained to her twin.

'Well... It's what Mom would have wanted,' Bobbie told her virtuously.

'Mom...! You haven't...' Samantha began but Bobbie shook her head.

'No. I'm leaving *that* to you—and Liam—not that... Oh...'

'What is it?' Samantha demanded hearing the surprised and excited note in her sister's voice as she looked towards the doorway.

'It's Gran and Gramps!' Bobbie exclaimed leaving her sister's side to hurry over to the doorway where Ruth and Grant were standing together with one of Ruth's nephews, Saul Crighton, his wife Tullah, and their children.

It was Saul's parents Hugh and Ann who Ruth and Grant had been staying with in Pembroke and as she stared at them Samantha shook her head and told Liam, 'I just don't believe this. All it needs now is for Mom and Pop to walk in through the door.'

'Well, I doubt that *that's* going to happen, but I think we ought to go over and make our explanations to your grandparents—or rather, I ought,' Liam told her ruefully.

Samantha shot him a surprised look. She could actually hear a faint note of almost boyish uncertainty in Liam's voice and there was quite definitely a slightly sheepish look in his eyes as he looked towards the group of people surrounding her grandparents. It was so unlike Liam to betray anything other than total self-confidence that such an unexpected display of vulnerability caused her to move closer to him and put her hand on his arm in a gesture that was almost protective.

'Gran will understand,' she told him. 'After all, she and Gramps…'

Abruptly Samantha stopped. What on earth was happening to her? Just for a moment it was almost as though she actually *was* Liam's fiancée, as though they *were* actually two very newly committed lovers catapulted into a very public arena they had never expected to have to enter at such an early stage in their newly discovered love. But it was too late now to withdraw from Liam. At the touch of her hand he had moved closer to her and she could see the way the others were regarding them. Infuriatingly Samantha discovered that she was actually blushing and, even worse, that she was more than happy to have the solid bulk of Liam to lean a little shyly into as he started to guide her across the floor to where her grandparents were waiting.

'So, it's finally happened! The two of you have stopped fighting long enough to fall in love.'

Samantha blinked as she heard the loving approval in her grandmother's voice and saw the happiness in her eyes.

'Liam, I just hope you know exactly what you're taking on,' Ruth was saying to Liam. 'You're *never* going to change her.'

'There's no way I'd want to,' Liam was replying in true lover-like fashion.

And, looking into his eyes heart-jerkingly for a breathless space of time, Samantha could almost believe he meant it.

The afternoon passed in a haze of hugs and kisses and congratulations, the Grosvenor rising to the occasion with true aplomb produced a buffet luncheon fit for the most discerning diner. Dizzily Samantha listened to the various

conversations humming in the air around her, the younger
ranks of the family were entertaining themselves in one
corner of the room whilst another group which included
Jon and Jenny had formed around Ruth and Grant, whilst
Bobbie, Luke, Tullah and Saul were also busy exchanging
reminiscences of their childhoods and of their own early
days as couples.

Of them all only Katie was partnerless. A calm very
private person, Katie, according to her mother Jenny, was
dedicated, not perhaps so much to her job but to the cause
it served.

Like Ruth, Katie had a very strong philanthropic caring
streak. Her work in the legal department of a large charity
might not be going to bring her either fame or fortune but
it had to give her a great deal of satisfaction, Samantha
acknowledged.

Not that Katie looked particularly happy right now
though, she admitted, or was it simply that the very cou-
pledness of everyone else there underlined the fact that
Katie was on her own.

When Saul and Tullah came over to congratulate them,
Tullah remarked teasingly, 'Perhaps you're going to beat
us to produce the first set of our generation of twin births,
after all...'

'Twins... With Liam running for the governorship I
doubt they're going to have time to conceive one child
never mind two,' Saul told his wife outspokenly.
Mortifyingly, whilst the other three laughed, Samantha
could feel herself starting to blush as though she were, in
reality, in love with Liam.

'When will you get married?' Tullah was asking. 'After
voting or...'

Liam gave Samantha a warning squeeze of her hand,

answering before she could say anything, 'We haven't settled on a date yet.'

'Well, I guess that means the end of your visit over here,' Bobbie commented ruefully several hours later when everyone else had gone bar Bobbie and Luke and their grandparents, Luke's parents having taken Francesca home with them for the night to give Bobbie some extra time to spend with her twin. She continued before Samantha could say anything,

'I know Liam can't stay over here very long and, of course, you're going to want to go back with him. When are you going to tell the folks?'

As Bobbie had already confided to Luke, the fact that Sam and Liam were lovers had proved to her how much her twin must love Liam.

'Sam has always been so picky—and never ever casually intimate with men in any kind of way—for her to have committed herself to Liam like this proves how much she loves him.'

'I don't need convincing,' Luke had responded knowingly. '*I* knew she and James wouldn't suit.'

'We're going to ring them just as soon as we can,' Liam answered for them both now.

'Well, I know that Sarah Jane won't be too surprised,' Ruth confounded Samantha by commenting. 'I know from what she's told me that she did have hopes...'

Her mother had *hopes...hopes* of her and Liam... How on earth could she have done? Samantha wondered bemusedly whilst Liam veiled his eyes.

He was not entirely surprised that Samantha's mother had guessed how he felt about her daughter. Mothers were, after all, notoriously very insightful in that way. Samantha herself, thank the Lord, was far less intuitive.

As he looked sideways at the ring glittering on Samantha's left hand he could almost taste the bittersweet flavour of the sharp cruelty of the gulf between the relationship the two of them were pretending to and reality.

He was still searingly aware of the double blow Samantha had given him in firstly accusing him of trying to use her to improve his chances of winning the vote—how could she think him capable of that kind of underhandedness?—and of secondly and even more hurtful telling him that she had cold-bloodedly decided to have sex with him because she wanted not *his* child but *a* child. That revelation hadn't just hurt him it had shocked him, as well.

The closeness of the Miller family had appealed to an idealism within Liam that he tried to keep hidden and protected and that Samantha, the woman he loved, should be prepared to deny her own child the kind of upbringing she herself had been so lovingly nurtured in was something he was finding hard to understand. And what he was finding even harder to understand or forgive was his own dangerous awareness that given a second opportunity to furnish Sam with the child she so much wanted, he doubted that he would be able to resist the temptation to do so; that way at least he'd have some kind of permanent tie with her…through their child.

As Samantha listened to her grandparents she acknowledged that her grandfather and Liam had always got on well. Grant's family was from the Deep South and he and Liam, in common with her father, shared a belief that it was of vital importance to find a way of integrating the diehards of both the Southern states and the Northern ones in a common purpose that would benefit everyone. Ruth and Liam had immediately taken to one another so that now, as the whole family, including Luke, began a passionate discussion about the increasingly urgent need to give those young people of both countries the incentive and the help to free themselves from what western journalists were currently referring to as 'the poverty trap,' momentarily Samantha felt somehow as though she was excluded from a particularly charismatic and exclusive circle.

Her views were not that much out of accord with those of the others, she recognised, it was just that she favoured a much more direct and possibly contentious method of putting them into operation.

'I guess it looks like we're going to be having dinner here,' Grant commented jovially at one point. 'We'd better book a table.'

Whilst the others were all eagerly assenting, only Liam hesitated, looking at Samantha and asking her in a quiet voice, 'You're very quiet, would you prefer to do something else?'

Samantha's eyes widened, a very definite tug of emotion dragging on her heart, a very real sense of warmth and happiness enveloping her. Liam at least had noticed that she wasn't joining in the others' enthusiastic discussion and he had felt *concerned* enough about her to ask what she wanted to do.

A small fluffy euphoric cloud materialised out of nowhere to wrap itself around her and cushion her. Instinctively she moved closer to Liam, virtually snuggling into his side without realising what she was doing. Not even the comforting strength of his arm going around her as he drew her even closer warned her of the danger she was courting or the vulnerability she was exposing, something which she later put down to the fact that she had, over the course of the afternoon, become so steeped in her role of newly affianced woman that playing that part had become second nature to her.

'Uh-huh…it looks to me like she would,' Bobbie teased her unmercifully, forcing Samantha to realise what she was doing and to push herself away from Liam as she denied fiercely, 'No…dinner here will be fine by me.'

'Well now, here's a thing,' Grant chuckled. 'It looks to me, Liam, like love is already taming our firebrand. She's even learning the art of tactful social fibbing. Perhaps she's not going to make such a bad Governor's wife, after all…'

'For your information,' Samantha began indignantly, her eyes flashing warning storm signals. But Liam silenced her quickly, leaning forward to kiss her briefly on the lips.

The dizziness that flooded her must be because she hadn't eaten much of the buffet, Samantha decided as she forced herself not to give in to the disturbing urge to wrap her arms around Liam and return his kiss—with interest—with very passionate interest.

'She's going to make a wonderful Governor's wife,' Liam told Grant throatily without taking his eyes off Samantha's face. 'And certainly the only wife that *this* potential Governor is *ever* going to want…'

Surrounded by the others' laughter Samantha tried to tear her gaze away from Liam's and discovered that she couldn't. She felt as though she were drowning, melting, as though her whole body was on fire…dissolving, aching, so much so that right now…

Her whole body went hot with mortified colour as she recognised just what direction her thoughts were taking and there was no use kidding herself, the urgent desire she had just felt flooding her body had nothing whatsoever to do with any maternal desire to make a baby. What was happening to her? When had acting the part of being in love with Liam, of having to pretend there was nothing she wanted more than to be alone with him...having to pretend that there was no one she wanted more than him, had right now become so easy, so natural, so *necessary*, that it was as automatic as just breathing?

Whilst the others fussed over practicalities Samantha sat in bemused silence.

'My, oh, my,' Grant commented jokingly at one stage later in the evening when Samantha hadn't even responded to the very obvious lure he had been trailing for her. 'I know they say that love changes a person but...'

To Samantha's surprise it was Liam who came to her rescue, shaking his head and saying firmly, 'Samantha's and my beliefs, our ideals, have never been as far apart as some folk like to think, it's just that my way of instituting them is a little less assertive than Sam's...'

Whilst the others were still laughing, he turned to her and picked up her left hand and carried it to his lips, kissing her ring finger in a gesture that was simple and loving and so totally without any kind of self-consciousness that Samantha felt her eyes smart with sharp tears. What would it be like if Liam really *did* love her? Previously her dreams of loving a man and being loved by him had all revolved around the family they would have. It had never occurred to her that she might feel such an overwhelming sense of bliss and security nor such a profound sense of belonging, of knowing that she could totally relax and allow someone else to carry her just for a little while.

Bemusedly she looked up into Liam's eyes. He was watching her with a mixture of gravity and an expression she couldn't define. All she knew was that it set her pulse rate rocketing and made her whole body go hot and sensitive just as though he had suddenly touched and caressed it.

Whilst the others were ordering their food he leaned towards her, closing the gap between them, and then whispered against her mouth, 'Keep on looking at me like that Samantha Miller and I might just forget all the reasons why this engagement of ours isn't for real and I might forget, too, just why those precautions I took last night so as not to get you pregnant were the right thing to do...'

And then he kissed her. Not just an ordinary little old kiss, either, but a long, slow, deeply passionate this is my woman and I love her kind of kiss, right there at the restaurant table with nearly all her family looking on. And, much as she loved them, just for a second Samantha wished very passionately that they weren't there and that Liam would do exactly what he had just been whispering to her that he wanted to do and that they were alone, upstairs, in his suite and that...

'You never did tell me what happened to James last night,' Bobbie announced, breaking the dangerous spell holding Samantha entranced.

'James...'

For a moment Samantha actually had difficulty in remembering who her sister meant. 'Oh, yes...well, he had...' She stopped, not sure how much she should say about just what had happened. After all, Rosemary was engaged to another man and she and James were supposed to thoroughly dislike one another.

'Er...there was a phone call,' Samantha fibbed in the end, 'and he said he had to leave.'

'It must have been fate,' Bobbie told her with a broad smile before adding in a semi-audible whisper, 'By the way, have you told Liam yet about you know what...'

'"You know what"?' Samantha frowned. 'I don't

know what you mean,' she began, but Bobbie stopped her, shaking her head and reminding her wickedly, 'Remember when you and I had our joint confession fest and I told you about my water fantasy and you…'

'Oh…yes…that…' Samantha headed her off quickly. There was no way she wanted Liam to hear about that idiotic sensual fantasy of hers about making love out of doors, not when they were not really a couple, not when he didn't, couldn't, really love her, but it was no use rolling an anguished look in her twin's direction and whilst Luke and their grandparents were engaged in their own conversation, Bobbie proceeded to inform Liam in a soft undertone just what Samantha's secret fantasy actually was.

'Bobbie, that was a teenage thing,' Samantha hissed, totally unable to bring herself to look at Liam to see how he was reacting to Bobbie's confidences.

'So were your feelings for Liam and now look what's happened,' Bobbie teased her unrepentantly.

It was late when they finally called the evening to an end, Luke and Bobbie leaving first and then Ruth and Grant following them within minutes.

'We'll talk tomorrow,' Bobbie had promised her sister before she left, adding, 'I know you'll want to fly back home with Liam but at least, with the two of you planning to get married it won't be very long before we're all together again.'

It was gone midnight when Samantha and Liam walked through the foyer towards the lifts.

'The hotel's emptied out a little now,' Liam informed her quietly as he buzzed for the lift, 'so I've been able to book you your own room.'

Her own room… Samantha tried to look appropriately

appreciative. Bobbie had thoughtfully returned home before the lunch and she had discreetly handed over to Samantha a large holdall containing some of her clothes and toiletries.

With the old-fashioned courtliness that had so often caused her to rebel against him in the past, Liam insisted on walking Samantha to her hotel room door and unlocking it for her. As she stepped past him into the room Sam had a wild longing to stop and turn straight into his arms.

The depth of her own longing unnerved her. What was happening to her? Surely she wasn't so easily suggestible that, less than twenty-four hours of playing at being Liam's lover and wife-to-be had made her feel so wrapped up in the role that she couldn't divorce herself from it and return to reality. She actually had to grit her jaw to stop herself from whispering to him that she wanted to spend the night in his room, in his bed, in his arms, and not just because she wanted his child—no, not just for that at all. What she wanted, she realised shakily, was Liam himself.

'We'll ring home in the morning,' Liam was saying to her.

It was as much as Samantha could trust herself to do to simply shake her head. If she opened her mouth, if she looked at him, if her body even thought that he might make the smallest move in her direction... Even after he had closed the door behind himself it was still several seconds before Samantha could trust herself to move; her fingers shook as she locked the door. The ring Liam had given her caught the light. Despite its weight she was barely aware of wearing it; it was almost as though it had always been there. Reluctantly she took it off. Her hand felt bare...naked...

It took a long time before she finally managed to drop

off to sleep and even then she didn't sleep very well. The
bed felt uncomfortable and empty without Liam in it...

Liam... Liam... Liam...

She sat upright, drawing up her knees and wrapping her
arms around them. What was happening to her? What *had*
happened to her? She had *never* been any good at pretending to feel or be what she did not. Never...and yet
today, pretending to be in love with Liam had come so
easily and naturally to her that—

Abruptly her body tensed as the unpalatable truth struck
her. Perhaps the pretence had been easy because, in reality, it was no pretence at all.

But how could that be? How could she possibly have
been in love with Liam without knowing it?

Perhaps she *had,* at some deep level of her subcon-
scious, known it. Perhaps that was why she had responded
to Liam the way she had. Perhaps that was why she had
been so consumed by the desire to conceive his child.
Nature worked in complex and not always totally clear
ways.

But she couldn't love Liam. *He* didn't love her. She
had had to learn that as a girl...and although she had
never admitted it even to Bobbie, accepting that he didn't
return her feelings had been one of the hardest and most
painful lessons she had ever had to bear. Her feelings for
him might have been those of an adolescent girl rather
than a woman, but that hadn't made them any the less
real. But Liam had made it stingingly clear that there was
no way he was going to allow her to dream hopeless
dreams about him and her pride had done the rest. Now
she knew she was going to need that same determination,
that same pride, again.

'Remember how very different you feel about all the
issues that are important to you,' Samantha warned her-

self, but listening to Liam this evening as he discussed his altruistic ambitions and hopes for the State she had been forced to acknowledge that, idealistically, they were not so very far apart, after all.

But what was she thinking? Even if by some miracle, Liam actually came to return her love, *she* would never in a million years ever make the kind of wife he was going to need. Even her own family were agreed on that although they seemed to think that she would change...compromise...but Samantha knew that she couldn't, not and still be true to herself.

She unclasped her knees and lay down again, silent tears dampening her pillow as she cried for the man she knew she could never share her life with and the babies they would never make together.

CHAPTER TEN

'SWEETHEART, isn't it exciting, the *Washington Post* is predicting that Liam is definitely going to win. Sam... what's wrong?' her mother asked anxiously as her comment failed to bring the reaction she had expected from her daughter.

'You're not still worrying about becoming the Governor's wife, are you?' she asked Samantha gently. 'Oh, but that's my fault. If I hadn't disliked it so much...' She paused and shook her head. 'But, Samantha, you are so much stronger than I am and even though you won't admit it, you *love* the kind of challenges you and Liam are going to be facing. People are already predicting that you're going to be the most progressive couple to ever hold state governorship, and your father is so very, very proud of you both.'

Samantha couldn't bring herself to look at her mother. Ever since her return with Liam some weeks ago it had been the same. Both her parents had been thrilled with their news and, despite the demands on her time with her father's impending retirement, her mother had still thrown herself into excited preparations for Samantha's wedding.

'We want to wait until after...after the inauguration,' Samantha had protested as she fought down the panicky feeling that was filling her but it seemed that the news of their engagement had started a roller coaster, a tidal wave of reaction, which once set in motion there was no way of stopping.

There had been rallies and meetings, interviews, TV

chat shows and such, a whole host of calls upon her time that Samantha in the end had had to concede that her father was right when he had advised her that she was going to have to put her career temporarily on hold at least until after the vote.

One unexpected consequence of her engagement had been the fact that Cliff had started to fawn over her in a way that she found totally nauseating, but now she had far, far more important things on her mind to worry about than him.

The stress she was under was beginning to tell. She had lost weight and the sparkle had gone from her eyes. Now the sapphire on her left hand looked a much deeper blue than they did. She and Liam hardly ever managed to get any time together such was the build-up towards the vote and so they had simply not had a chance to discuss how and when they were going to break the news that they had decided, after all, that they did not love one another.

Samantha closed her eyes. And that was another lie she was going to have to learn to live with. Liam might not love her but *she* certainly loved him. Oh, how she loved him. Her eyes burned with anguished tears.

'Sam, sweetheart, what is it?' her mother begged anxiously as she hurried over to wrap her arms around her.

'It's nothing,' Samantha fibbed. 'I guess everything's become so pressured and...'

'...and Liam isn't here and you miss him. Honey, I *do* know,' her mother consoled her. 'But never mind, he'll be back this weekend and the two of you should be able to get some time on your own. Oh, and by the way, I thought we might fly into New York the weekend after and check out some wedding gowns.'

Wedding gowns. Samantha's heart gave a frantic bound. There was nothing she wanted to do more than walk down the aisle on her father's arm and to have Liam waiting there at the altar for her. Nothing... But that was just an impossible dream...a totally impossible dream.

When Liam rang her later that day, for once she was on her own and able to tell him quickly, 'Liam, we've got to talk.'

There was a small pause and she guessed he was probably not on his own by the guarded tone in his voice as he responded, 'Uh-huh...is something wrong?'

'Mom's talking about us going to New York the weekend after next to look at wedding gowns,' she told him, hoping he would be able to decode the message contained in what she was saying. 'She thinks we ought to be discussing which of the Crighton cousins we will be having as attendants and she wants me to go upstate to visit with Dad's family there to see what furniture we might want to get out of store. You know when Dad's folks passed away that Bobbie and I were left some antique furniture and that it's still in store.' She was starting to babble, Samantha recognised as she forced herself to take a deep calming breath.

There was a family business in New England, as well, that her father intended returning to.

Liam, although he never really discussed it, having sold his father's business, was a comfortably wealthy man, probably even more wealthy than her own parents, but money for its own sake had never interested Samantha.

One of the innovative measures Liam wanted to bring in if he was elected was a special form of scholarship for young people who otherwise would not have been able to afford to go to college and he had told Samantha that he intended to underwrite such scholarships himself from his own private means.

The political gap between them was closing with what

for Samantha was a heart-wrenching speed. Now she could not even cling to her ideals as a reason to stop loving him.

'I'll be home at the weekend,' she heard Liam saying quietly in response to her call. 'We can talk then.'

The weekend. Wearily Samantha replaced the receiver. That was two whole days away yet. So, for two more whole days, forty-eight hours, she was still going to be Liam's wife-to-be. After that… After that she would need to go as far away from him as she could…to go somewhere where she could hide away and learn to live with her loss and her pain.

A forlorn look darkened Samantha's eyes as she studied the photograph in the article she had just been reading. It depicted her and Liam. They were seated together in the library of the Governor's house, Liam's arm resting tenderly around her shoulders whilst she was turning slightly towards him, her lips gently parted as though in anticipation of his kiss. It was a photograph of two lovers, two people who couldn't wait to be alone together, and it had been taken to accompany the article alongside it in which Liam had been interviewed about his plans for the state should he be elected into office.

And they said the camera didn't lie. Since her telephone conversation with Liam the previous day Samantha had been mentally rehearsing just what she was going to say to him when he returned. Being Liam, he would be bound to demand to know why it was so urgently imperative that their pseudo engagement was brought to an immediate end and, of course, there was no way that she could tell him, so she would have to invent a reason and so far she had not managed to come up with one which she knew would convince him.

So why not tell him the truth? Quickly she got up and walked across her room and stood staring unseeingly down into the garden that her mother loved so much.

She had got up early this morning and left before breakfast, having told her mother the previous evening that she needed a little time on her own and promising that, yes, she would go and look over the furniture stored in the depository whilst she was here in her father's home town, the same New England town that her parents intended to come back to when his term of office had ended.

This house was old by New England standards, although in Crighton terms it would no doubt have been termed relatively new. She and Bobbie had grown up in this quiet traditional town and their family was a part of it. If she were to go into the town now people would stop her and ask her not just about her parents but about her sister and her sister's child, as well. They would ask after her brother Tom, currently at college and destined to take over the family business from her father when ultimately he stepped down from its overall control—in the time whilst her father had been State Governor he had had to appoint a deputy to take care of the day-to-day running of the business but he had still retained overall responsibility for it.

Tell Liam the truth! How simple it sounded but how totally impossible that would be. Even if she could bear to expose herself to the humiliation of actually telling him that she loved him…him a man who never could and never would return those feelings, how could she be sure that in telling him she wasn't somehow subconsciously trying to put emotional pressure on him to feel sorry for her, to take pity on her and to… To what? To marry her because she loved him? *No!* Immediately she shrank from the very thought. *No! No.* That was the last thing she

wanted. If only she had a less volatile and more phleg-
matic personality she might be able to contain her feelings
a little better, to simply stoically wait out things until after
the election, but the day-to-day effect of playing a false
role was beginning to rasp so painfully on her nerves that
she knew she couldn't trust herself to somehow betray the
truth.

No, their engagement would have to be brought to an
official end with a proper public announcement that they
had both decided that they had made a mistake.

Out of the corner of her eye she saw a car turning into
the drive to the house. Her heart started to hammer heavily
as she recognised it.

It was Liam's.

Liam!

What was he doing *here?* There was still another
twenty-four hours to go before he was due back.

Quickly she started to hurry downstairs, dragging open
the heavy front door just as he reached it.

The house, although not presently lived in, was cleaned
twice a week but it still had that sad lonely air to it that
unlived-in homes possess, Samantha reflected as she
closed the door behind Liam and demanded shakily,
'Liam, what are you doing here? You said you wouldn't
be back until tomorrow.'

'I know but...you didn't sound too good when we
spoke and when I rang this morning and your mother told
me that you'd left early to come over here, I decided to
cancel the rest of my meetings and drive over.'

'You cancelled your meetings because of *me.*'
Samantha looked at him in surprise. Although Liam's ambition was more of the steely determined sort than the
aggressive go-getting type, she was still surprised that he
had been concerned enough to behave so impulsively.

'Your mother says you aren't eating…'

'I've got a lot on my mind,' Samantha told him defensively. 'I guess I just don't feel that hungry. Liam…I…' She stopped and then took a deep breath, turning away from him so that she wouldn't have to look at him whilst she told him, so that he couldn't look at her and see the truth in her eyes, because she knew that if he did she couldn't bear to see the corresponding pity in his.

'I can't go on with this… It's got to end. The longer we leave it the worse it's going to get. Mom's already making plans for our wedding and Dad…' She stopped and swallowed.

'They're going to hate me for us not getting married. I never realised…' She stopped again. 'We've got to tell them that we've changed our minds, Liam, and that it's over.'

He was silent for so long that in the end she had to turn round and look at him, but although she searched his face for some clue in his expression that would tell her what he was feeling and thinking she could see none.

'It would never have worked out anyway,' she told him, forcing herself to try to make a joke of it. 'Can you really see me as a Governor's wife?'

'Yes, as a matter of fact I can.'

Open-mouthed, Samantha stared at him, unable to conceal her reaction from him.

'But you've always said how impossible I would be and…'

'No. *You've* always said how impossible you would be,' Liam corrected her. 'And maybe twenty, even ten years ago you would have been right. The restrictions imposed on *you* to ensure *my* success *would* have been impossible for you to bear and such that no one would have had the right to want to impose them on you, but things have changed Samantha and are still changing.

'We're living in a new world, a world that's coming to not just see but to welcome and embrace all manner of different kinds of thinking and all manner of different views. We're a strong, braver people now, and we no longer feel threatened by new ideas or innovative ways of dealing with problems. The kind of Governor I intend to be would never have been tolerated a decade ago. The men and women we'll be representing are people like ourselves, the men know that their roles have to be interchangeable with those of their partners and, men and women alike, they recognise that the old style of a woman "standing by her man" has gone, that now both partners in a relationship have the right to expect support from the other, that *both* partners are equal and mutually supportive of one another, that a woman has as much right to expect her man to stand by her as he does her.

'We're on the threshold of a new era, Sam, and I predict that it's one that will allow people to coexist in harmony as individuals and that the old straitjackets which required people to conform to certain rigid patterns will be swept aside as people overcome their fears and prejudices to accept one another as they are, to respect them as they are...

'No, you may not have made a good *traditional* Governor's wife, the kind that was always there two steps behind her husband and faded into the wallpaper, but that isn't the kind of wife *I've* ever wanted. I want a wife who will be my partner in every sense of the word and she'll be standing there right alongside me and sometimes I guess, right in front of me,' Liam concluded, almost humorously.

For a moment Samantha was too moved to speak.

Everything he had said had touched her so emotionally that she knew she was frighteningly close to breaking down and telling him exactly how she felt about him. How could she *not* love him now, after what he had just said.

'Do the voters know about all this?' she managed to joke shakily.

'The voters have no role to play in my private relationship with you, Sam. Besides,' he added quietly, 'it may have been true that I did once think of you as a woman too individual by far to conform to being a politician's wife, but I was wrong. It wasn't you who needed to change your thinking but me who needed to change mine, and I have done, Sam. I don't just love you, I admire and respect you, as well. There's nothing about you I could ever want to change—not one single thing—apart, of course, from changing your name to mine!' Liam told her in a slow smoky voice that made her stomach tie itself in knots and her heart turn somersaults inside her chest.

Oh, why, why was he doing this to her...? Why couldn't he just agree with what she had said and walk away from her?

'Uh...but we don't *have* a private relationship,' she told him huskily. 'It's just pretend, Liam...it's...'

'Is it?' he challenged her, and then the next minute she was in his arms and he was holding her, kissing her gently at first and then when he felt the soft tremulous response of her lips and the betraying shudder of pleasure that racked through her with a fierce hungry passion that had all Samantha's objections dying unspoken. All she could do, all she *wanted* to do was to simply cling to him; respond to him, *give* him all the love in her that was bursting to be expressed.

'If the voters can't see what an asset you'd be, what a

gift you are, then that's their loss,' she could hear Liam saying thickly to her as he cupped her face and looked down into her eyes with such a blaze of love in his that Samantha felt as though its heat was going to melt her right through to her toes.

'And their loss isn't going to be mine. Rather than lose you I'd step down from the race.'

Samantha's eyes widened. She could see in his eyes, hear in his voice, that he meant exactly what he was saying.

'You'd do *that*…for *me*…' she whispered.

'For you *and* for us,' Liam told her softly. 'If that's the only way I can convince you that you mean more to me than anything or anyone else…'

'Oh, Liam…' Tenderly Samantha touched his face with her fingertips. 'I guess that must mean that you love me,' she told him dreamily, her tears falling on his skin.

'Just why the hell else would I come racing across the Atlantic like a complete fool,' Liam challenged her gruffly. 'Have you *any* idea what it did to me to hear you telling me that you were going to go get yourself an English husband…an English *father* for your kids…'

'But I didn't *know*. You *never* said.'

'*You* never *wanted* me to say,' Liam retorted. 'You treated me like…like I might have been your brother.'

'That was because…well, when you first came to work for Dad you made it plain that you were strictly off limits and…'

'You were still a kid…a baby…' Liam interrupted her. 'And then, later, when you grew up, you just didn't seem to want to know.'

'I didn't know,' Samantha admitted, 'not until…' She stopped and blushed a little and then laughed. 'I guess I had to go to bed with you to find out just exactly what I *do* feel for you.'

'Uh-huh… So it *wasn't* just to get me to help you make a baby then,' he reminded her.

Samantha shook her head.

'I guess I had to tell myself it was because I was so shocked by what I had done, but deep down inside I think I must always have known…have felt… That Sunday at the Grosvenor when all the family were there it felt so good, so *right*—us being together. I missed you so that night.'

'Nowhere near as much as I missed you,' Liam groaned as he took hold of her.

As he started to kiss her she snuggled closer to him, eagerly responding to his rising passion, but then suddenly she pulled away from him and demanded softly, 'Liam, is there really nothing you wouldn't do for me…?'

'Nothing,' he responded. 'Why, what is it you want…?'

'Well, this time…' She stopped and flushed prettily. 'This time when we make love, could I have…could we… I want your baby, Liam,' she told him.

'Liam!' she protested as he started to kiss her with devastating intensity, running his hands possessively the length of her torso, cupping her breasts and then pulling her so tightly into his own body that she could feel the powerful throb of his arousal.

'What*ever* you want from me you can have, *whenever* you want it,' he told her rawly. 'But when it comes to making babies…' He cupped the back of her head and massaged the flesh, looking deep into her eyes.

'I think we both know that that's something we want to happen *after* we're married and not because of what anyone *else* might think but because we want *our* kids to grow up knowing that we loved and respected one another to want to give them that security.'

'Oh, Liam…' Samantha sighed blissfully as she melted into his arms. 'Oh, Liam…'

The house was fully furnished with beds in every room, but Samantha knew that, right now, it wouldn't have mattered *where* they were, so compellingly and urgent was their need and their hunger for one another. Just the touch of Liam's breath on her bare skin was enough to send her body into tiny shivers of almost orgasmic pleasure and as for *his* reaction when she touched and kissed him.

'So, you want to hold out until we're married,' she teased him at one point, and in the end they both admitted it was a very near-run thing.

Their wedding took place three weeks before her father's official retirement and six before Liam's inauguration as the state's new Governor and, of course, during her father's speech there were several jokes about him losing a daughter but gaining a Governor's wife in the family.

Later, when she stood next to her mother, her sister and her brother as their father received the thanks of the state officials for what he had done for the state and then, later still when she stood beside Liam whilst her father spoke of his pride in knowing just what Liam would achieve, she was filled with such pride for the man she had married that she felt that her heart would burst with it. But her most special memory of all as she listened to Liam giving his acceptance speech and discreetly patted the still flat smoothness of her stomach and whispering to their growing child to listen to its daddy, she was thinking not of the future but of the very special and private occasion when the baby growing inside her was conceived.

'You'll love it,' Liam had insisted when she had made

a face and exclaimed in horror when he told her that their brief honeymoon was not to be in some idyllic tropical paradise, but a back-packing trip into the mountains.

But the few days they had spent there had proved to be far more memorable than any luxury surroundings could ever have been, especially the first night they had made camp in the small secret glade Liam had taken her to right beside a spring-fed small mountain pool. They had swum there together naked, the water icy cold against the heat of their skin, and then they had made love beneath the stars with their benign silvery glow the only witness to Samantha's soft cries of pleasure as their bodies merged together and created the new life she was now carrying.

The whole family had come over for the wedding, every single one of them, including Bobbie proudly bearing her newborn son, and Samantha had noticed again how withdrawn and quiet Katie had been.

'Jenny is very concerned about her,' Ruth had told them. 'She works so hard, too hard, Jenny thinks. I've suggested that she ought to try to persuade Katie to move back to Haslewich. They could do with her help in the family-run practice.'

Samantha, who had seen the hopeless, helpless look in Katie's eyes whenever they rested on her twin and her husband, wasn't so sure that it was just hard work that was affecting Katie but she kept her thoughts to herself. The family suspected that Louise might be pregnant, but nothing had been said yet. Samantha couldn't imagine anything worse than to love one's twin's man. She couldn't imagine how she would have coped if, for instance, Bobbie and Liam had fallen in love. Just to have the thought form inside her head was enough to make her go dizzy at the thought of the pain such a situation would bring.

James, too, had attended their wedding looking slightly sheepish and keeping his distance from her. Not that he had any need to do so, she had no right to demand an explanation from him for that kiss she had seen him and Rosemary exchanging. But Rosemary's fiancé certainly did. Now Samantha looked across the room to where Liam was working at his desk and then got up and walked over to him, taking up a teasing provocative pose as she perched beside him, swinging the long length of her legs.

'Well now, Mr. Governor, sir,' she breathed sexily, 'they say that power is a very sexy aphrodisiac and that powerful men are very, very sexy in bed.' As she spoke she was reaching across and starting to unfasten his shirt. 'Would you say that that was true…'

Liam leaned back in his chair and closed his eyes and then teased her, 'Well, I guess there's only one way you're going to know,' before getting up and taking hold of her hand and asking her, 'Have I told you today how much I love you, Samantha Connolly?'

'Mmm…not since breakfast,' Samantha responded.

'Mmm… Well I do…and I always will.'

'*Always*…even when I'm hugely pregnant,' Samantha asked him.

'Especially then,' Liam told her softly. 'Oh, yes, most especially then.'

It was perfect. Life was perfect. Their love was perfect. Liam was perfect. The perfect man, the perfect husband…the perfect father…and she loved him more than she would ever, ever be able to find all the words to say.

* * * * *

Look for Katie Crighton's story, A Perfect Night. *Coming Soon!*

Coming Next Month

HARLEQUIN PRESENTS®

THE BEST HAS JUST GOTTEN BETTER!

#2097 THE MARRIAGE DEAL Helen Bianchin
When Michael Lanier had made his wife choose between her career and their marriage, she'd left him. Now Sandrine's career was facing a crisis, and only Michael could help her. He would do so, but for a price: Sandrine must agree to share his bed and his life once more!

#2098 THEIR ENGAGEMENT IS ANNOUNCED Carole Mortimer
To avoid his mother's matchmaking, Griffin Sinclair had announced that he was going to marry Dora Baxter. She had to play along—but it wasn't going to be easy, as Dora had secretly been in love with Griffin for years....

#2099 AUNT LUCY'S LOVER Miranda Lee
In order to gain her inheritance, Jessica had to live in her aunt Lucy's house for a month with Sebastian—described in Lucy's will as her "loyal and loving companion." But could this blond hunk really have been her aunt's *lover*?

#2100 EMERALD FIRE Sandra Marton
Having fallen for Slade McClintoch's powers of seduction once before, Brionny was afraid of making the same mistake again. And she couldn't be sure if he was really interested in her, or if he was simply trying to discover her precious secret....

#2101 THE UNEXPECTED WEDDING GIFT Catherine Spencer
Ben Carreras is astounded when an old flame gate-crashes his wedding insisting he's the father of the baby boy in her arms and that he must take his son. But how can Ben break this bombshell to his new bride...?

#2102 A HUSBAND'S VENDETTA Sara Wood
Although Luc Maccari's marriage to Ellen had been blistered with passion, she'd abandoned him when he needed her most. Now Ellen was back, and Luc wanted revenge. But seducing Ellen reminded him of what he'd been missing, too—and then he discovered her heartrending secret....

CNM0400